sentimental,

heartbroken

rednecks

stories

Greg Bottoms

Context Books *New York*

sentimental,

heartbroken

rednecks

All rights reserved under International and Pan-American Copyright Conventions.
Published in the United States of America
Context Books, New York.
Distributed by Publishers Group West

www.contextbooks.com

Portions of this book, in slightly different form, have appeared in *Alaska Quarterly Review*, *Another Chicago Magazine*, *The Beacon Best of 1999*, *Boldtype*, *Creative Nonfiction*, *Exquisite Corpse*, *Mississippi Review*, *Nerve*, and *Prism International*. The author would like to thank the editors of these magazines and anthologies.

Special thanks to Jenny Bent and Beau Friedlander

Designer: Cassandra Pappas
Jacket design: Carol Devine Carson
Typeface: Monotype Bembo

Context Books
368 Broadway
Suite 314
New York, NY 10013

Library of Congress Cataloging-in-Publication Data

Bottoms, Greg.
    Sentimental, heartbroken rednecks : stories / Greg Bottoms.
        p.   cm.
    ISBN 1-893956-15-6
    1. Southern States—Social life and customs—Fiction.   I. Title.
PS3602.O88 S46 2001
813'.6—dc21

                                                                    2001002863

9 8 7 6 5 4 3 2 1

Manufactured in the United States of America

I tried to save the world, but it didn't work out.

—Richard Selzer

contents

sentimental,

heartbroken

rednecks

nostalgia for ghosts

i.

*A*s *a small boy,* I suffered from extreme fevers. They came like phantoms,
burning through me, blurring my vision. They
covered me in cold sweat, ridding me of food and
liquid and waste until I was aware—without the
reserves of language or the ability to name my fears
and feelings—of a new kind of existence, an emptiness and lightness of body.

The fevers always began accompanied by fear
and anxiety—the same dread that animates dreams
of falling—at times so forceful that I thought I
would suffocate, dying on an old, worn-out couch
or on the cold bathroom tile. Once my tempera-

ture settled, though, topping out at 103 or 104 degrees, there was a sickly ease holding me, as if I'd stepped into another world.

High temperatures came first from the croup: deep, painful coughs like lightning strikes at the solar plexus, threatening to split me in half. Later there were middle-ear infections: buzzings in my head, the outside world muffled through antihistamines and painkillers. Then came bronchitis: a tightening in the chest, a lack of oxygen, mucus rising like an organic sludge from the bottom of my lungs until every sound from me came wrapped in a bubbling wetness.

Some of my clearest memories, existing with a near-photographic clarity untrammeled by the erosive nature of time, are of my mother holding me through long winter nights over a steaming sink or bathtub as I stared blankly, dreamily, crazily at the dirt- and mold-spotted mortar between the tiles of the room. She would drape a towel over both our heads so that I would breathe only steam. In a sonorous, calming voice she would sing and shush as we rocked, until, miraculously it seemed to me, she had saved me from dying again—a thirty-year-old heroine in a tattered robe and shaggy slippers, the purple half-moons of exhaustion, of complete parental depletion, weighing down her eyes—

opening up my bronchi so that I could breathe, maybe even sleep.

In the morning we would be at the doctor's office again, where both the horror and the strange magic of sickness would be temporarily destroyed.

ii.

I routinely saw ghosts during the heights of illness and fever. I stop on this memory. Surely it is false. But perhaps that is not the point—truth or falsity. Whether the ghosts were figments or not, my visions of them, and my steadfast belief as a boy in the reality of these visions, were real, as truthful as anything I can think of, perhaps more so because of their force, the space they take up in my memory.

When the fevers came, I would lie nearly paralyzed by fatigue and a sort of slow-motion hysteria in my dark room in our small, brick house in Tidewater, Virginia. Crickets and frogs complained through the open windows. And I waited for shadows in the shape of the dead to walk through my bedroom door. Ghosts would stop, three paces in— always three paces: one, two, three—then vanish, each dark phantom becoming the next, like images bleeding together in a kaleidoscope.

iii.

On Sundays, my family would go to the Methodist Church near our home, often walking there along the edges of cornfields, through a path in the woods, across vacant, overgrown lots. I didn't mind going to church then (though I stopped attending completely as a teenager, when I discovered alcohol and marijuana and what I thought of as the liberating sounds of the Sex Pistols and X, among others), because the stories of Christ and the apostles, of miracles and magic and the inexplicable, were usually interesting and well told.

One Sunday, after a long week of illness and fevers, during the season of Lent, when the church was filled with purple cloth and white flowers, I first heard, or first really listened to, the story of Christ rising from the dead. Though this was certainly the most intriguing story thus far at church, beating out even Job and his boils, or Moses parting the Red Sea or the burning bush, or Christ conjuring food and drink from virtually nothing to sate the hungry masses, what made it profound to me was that it explained the ghosts that I saw with every high fever. People, people who lived on the earth long ago or shortly ago, died, and were buried; but then, because Christ made it so, they rose from the dead and continued living, many of them for some reason stopping by my room.

To my mother sitting beside me in the pew I said, —I can see people like Jesus.

She looked at me. —What? she whispered.

—In my bedroom sometimes. There are people like Jesus.

—Sshh, she said, her hand resting heavily on my leg. —Don't say things like that.

iv.

A young girlfriend, Debra, the person I spent most of my time with on the weekends and in the summer, lived three doors down in a brick one-story on a quarter-acre grass lot identical, almost, to my family's. She was adopted, as was her brother. Her father went jogging one day. He was forty, overweight. It was one of those heat waves you expect in the South—steaming asphalt, a weight to the sunlight, midday silences, mirages of water receding on the highways where the smell of melting rubber lingered. He had a massive heart attack on the sidewalk near my home. People came out, tried to help; paramedics were called. But it was too late. In a neighborhood where he had lived for nearly fifteen years, a neighborhood in which real estate values were plummeting because of enforced busing, racial unrest, and spiking crime rates against person and property, his heart had clenched tight as a locked jaw and quit.

I saw it happen. Or I think I saw it happen. In my memory there is a space reserved for the image of his collapsing: he is tying his shoe, then putting his ear to the root-cracked concrete to listen closely to a faint rumbling underground, then lying down to rest, to sleep.

Weeks later, after the funeral and the still silence of mourning that engulfed their house, I told Debra not to worry, that death was a door. People were still around, and mostly fine, and sometimes, when I was sick, I could see them. I buttressed my story with talk of God and Jesus, of Mary Magdalene, of the giant stone rolled away, of the empty tomb, the triumphant light of holiness and salvation. I now knew a story that could make everything better. I believed that somehow made me powerful, impervious to life's ultimate tragedies.

v.

Getting off the bus one day—I was seven—I watched as a girl in a wheelchair, with a miniature body and a normal, adult-sized head, made as if to cross the busy highway just outside of our subdivision, where the bus dropped off the neighbor-hood kids on the wide sidewalks. The day was hazy, steamed up around the edges like a televised dream. The girl couldn't see around the bus—a wall of yellow, the roar of cars. Probably she was mentally as well as physically impaired.

When the car hit her, she was thrown high into the air, coming down, lifeless, on the street's grass median. The bluntness of the moment was a shock, like a hammer to the face. There was something false about it. It lacked narrative, lacked the simple decency of making sense. It was nothing like TV. No swelling of triumphant or tragic music. No fog effects, or noirish shadows around the body, no commentators spouting irony or melodrama or some sophisticated mixture of both. No chalk lines to be drawn. No dissonant guitar chords, or quick cuts toward overly weighted symbols, or a dark-ening screen to pull it all together. I'd gotten used to death as it was presented by the experts, people who'd studied the science of human perceptions, who knew about narrative formulas and the math-ematics of audience emotions. Now Debra's father and this—what?—midget? Dwarf? Death hap-pened in the blink of an eye; then it was over, a life expelled—so simple as to seem degrading, the degradation so venal as to almost necessitate an af-terlife.

The bus driver, a large woman with strange configurations of moles like stellar constellations on her face, sent all the kids away. Then there were cops, paramedics, a quickly forming crowd. Someone was shouting and shouting and shouting, but you couldn't understand any of it because the language was bent by panic, embroidered with loss, rising up and up and dissipating like factory smoke over our replicated houses.

At home, feeling numb and tingly, jarred and electrified, my spine fairly humming from adrenaline, still not quite believing what I saw to be real, I vomited. I couldn't tell my mother what happened. I couldn't find the breath, the right words. She heard about it from Debra's mother. She tried to cheer me up, to make me forget, with sweet talk and rubbing and promises of treats and cartoons.

I didn't go to school for the rest of the week, complaining, falsely, of an intense stomachache, staring blankly at cartoons all morning (Wile E. Coyote dying and coming back, dying and coming back), running errands in the afternoon with my mother—the beauty salon, the drugstore, the post office—seeing, on the periphery of my vision, the dead girl rising up in shop windows. I noticed people in wheelchairs everywhere. I suddenly lived in a city of deformities—something wrong with the air here, the water. I had a strange feeling that if I went back on the bus I would be sentenced to see something like that every day. I wondered if during the next fever the little girl—or tiny adult—would roll through my darkened doorway, the bent wheels of her chair squeaking and clanking.

vi.

But I did go back to school. Eventually I had to.

My best friend there was a black boy named Barry Fox. He was the funniest, smartest kid I knew, a true comedian with timing well beyond his elementary years. He said things to kids like: *Your momma's so fat she leaves a ring around the pool. Your momma's so fat she has to butter the bathtub to turn over. Your momma's ass got its own zip code.*

One Monday, early in the spring, Barry didn't come to school. He didn't come on Tuesday or Wednesday either. On Thursday he showed up again but didn't say anything. Finally, at lunch, he told me that his nineteen-year-old uncle, who lived with him and his mother and sisters in the Pine Chapel "projects," had been stabbed to death in a fight. I could tell he was about cry.

Again, in an effort to console, I told the story

about my power to see the dead when I was sick.
I tried to reassure him by telling him about Christ's
resurrection.

—What the hell you sayin', he almost shouted.
He was suddenly furious, telling me that I didn't
know a thing about his uncle, or about Jesus, or
about his family, or about black people, or about
anything at all. He said that his dead-ass uncle
wouldn't be let into my white-ass house anyway,
dead or alive.

He was right.

Then he told me he hated me. Then he did cry,
right into his open hands.

vii.

I needed a fever to prove to myself that this was
real, that I could see what I thought, what I believed, I could see.

But it was spring, harder to get truly, deathly ill
when the weather was beautiful and warm. And—
both blessing and curse, I thought—I seemed to
be getting heartier, healthier; I was getting bigger
and stronger, even good at sports.

I did have some close calls with fevers that
spring, though.

viii.

I would often go over to the Drabble's house.
They were strict Southern Baptists. The father was
a mechanic, as mean and quick to violence as any
man I have ever been around; the mother stayed
home with the nine children, ranging in age from
four to eighteen. The children were not allowed
to swim; the boys could not wear short sleeves or
short pants; the girls wore floor-length handmade
dresses and were not allowed to cut their hair,
ever, their astounding manes cascading down below their waists. My family lived cramped in our
small house with only four. They lived in a house
considerably smaller than ours with eleven, which
meant things tended to spill outside.

What spilled out of the house were the beatings.
The father would take the boys out and beat them
with his fists, rubbing their faces down into the
dirt of the yard. The girls he would beat with a
leather belt as he swung them around the yard by
their hair or shirt or arm, each girl screaming at a
slightly different pitch.

Usually, though, Mr. Drabble was not home
weekdays.

I went to the Drabble's because they were, due
to the pressures of their strict upbringing, I imagine, the worst kids I'd ever known—a whole new

species of bad. The boys had pornographic magazines and shot BB guns at neighboring houses; they
smoked cigarettes and drank stolen liquor in the
woods. The oldest boy, who recently had a bullet
shot into the door of his primer-colored El Ca-
mino "by a motherfucking spook," always had pot
and an assortment of pills.

The other thing that spilled out of their existence into the yard, piling up in the backyard, was
junk. A paradise of junk. Because the father was a
mechanic, a poor mechanic, a do-it-yourselfer, a
fixer-upper, he brought home old engines and
minibikes and motorcycle parts and steering wheels
and hood ornaments and tires and bent rims and
smashed-in doors and washing machines and re-
frigerators and forklift parts.

One day, Rodney, the youngest boy, a boy who
had learned much from his father, began throwing
heavy hubcaps into the air, seeing if he could ac-
cidentally smash one of his sisters' skulls. One came
down onto my head and knocked me nearly un-
conscious. It sounded like an alarm went off in my
brain.

Later, with my mother again tending to me, I
felt nauseated, with a mild concussion, and I
thought that perhaps a fever would follow. But,
disappointingly, it didn't.

A few weeks after this, on a blustery afternoon

after a large northeaster had brushed the East Coast, taking out trees and light poles and local fishing piers, some kids and I were playing during a church social and cookout with an army parachute, the origin of which escapes me, but I imagine it had made its way from Vietnam into some kid's attic.

We devised a game. The wind was thunderous. The wind was an angry scream. You could let the parachute fill and it would tug several children holding onto the ropes along through a field, laughing and screaming.

The game was who could hold on the longest before the old parachute came to rest in a copse of trees. Being the winner of this game meant that I floated up over the field, up over the world, seeing broken bottles and abandoned tires and dog feces whizzing by beneath me, until, at a speed of ten or fifteen miles per hour, I went slamming through saplings and ultimately into a large pine tree.

For a moment, the wind knocked out of me, I felt close to death, nearly smiling to myself through my grimace and tears because I felt that nausea and vomiting, sure signs of a fever, were on their way. But I was seven, strangely able to shake off even the harshest physical traumas with nothing more than a good cry. I was eating Brunswick stew within the hour, singing Good News Bible hymns.

Greg Bottoms

ix.

When my mother was out of the kitchen I began sticking my head in the refrigerator, having heard that cold air on your head brought on sickness. I ate soap; I ate a whole can of years-old liverwurst I found in the back of my grandmother's pantry because I'd once thrown up after doing so on a dare. I tried eating my grandmother's chitlins (pig's large intestines, fried). Nothing, nothing, nothing. I feared I'd never see the ghosts again.

x.

Summer evaporated. Fall arrived, with the sad news that we would be moving to a much nicer place, where only solidly middle-class white people lived. My father was going to stretch himself financially to get us out of this neighborhood, this city, and this school district that he believed were crumbling all around us.

Our impending move, our moving up in the world, was devastating news. I needed the fevers to see the ghosts; I also, I believed, needed the exactly perfect darkness of my bedroom in the hissing silence of night.

xi.

The first cold snap came with rain and wind. I was down the street at Debra's, who often asked me if I had seen her father. It wasn't for her, really, but for her mother, who no longer left the house, who just sat at the kitchen table in her bathrobe, drinking instant coffee, staring at the chipped Formica.

Rain tapped on the windows of Debra's room. Grayness coated everything.

I left their house and, through pouring rain and cold wind, walked across the fields near the church, out into the woods. I stayed there for several hours, praying. I didn't know how to pray then, not really, not in the way I would learn years later, when I was angry and unmoored and broken, but I gave it my best, most earnest try. I leaned against a tree in the weird bright darkness, shivering and soaked, asking God to make me sick, to make me almost dead, to show me one more time that life was not just this, not just simply this. I prayed until I heard my mother and father shouting, a bit frantic-sounding, from our backyard.

Within forty-eight hours, I had the flu, a middle-ear ache, and the beginnings of the most virulent case of bronchitis I have ever suffered through.

My fever spiked at nearly 105 degrees before dropping back to 102. I slept in an icy tub for an hour, dreaming of carousels and lawn ornaments and ladders and wild cats and my mother's voice miles and miles and miles away.

xii.

Then it was night again. I remained still in my bed. My head throbbed with every heartbeat. My mouth held the corroding taste of sickness. The darkness was perfect. I waited for Debra's father, or Barry's uncle, or the miniature, deformed girl in the squeaking and clanking wheelchair, or someone, anyone who had died, ever. I stared into the blackness. I leaned forward. Out my window, out in the real world, a car horn was bleating, and a dog was barking, and someone, somewhere, was falling asleep.

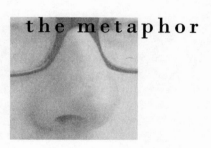

the metaphor

Preliminary Report

*E*llis, a twenty-seven-year-old black neigh-bor the young writer never met or spoke to, was shot in the stomach by a rookie police offi-cer and killed. This happened when the writer was twenty-three, unemployed. His neighborhood in Richmond, Virginia, was low-rent, mixed race—the only place he could afford. He had bars on his windows. He had $56.74, according to his journal. He had a mattress, some clothes, some books, some CDs. He did not, now, have much else. Except for time on his hands, curiosity.

Fact 1

When Ellis was shot he had been fleeing the scene of what resembled a robbery. The shooting was the reason the two guys in front of the writer's apartment—Ellis's former friends and roommates at the same halfway—were torturing the old, abandoned couch.

Evidence 1

The couch: The couch slumped three-legged on the cracked, weed-sprouting sidewalk—yellow, filthy, full of holes and protruding springs like rusty antennae. Drunks and runaways often slept on it; prostitutes, male and female and males dressed as females, rested on it, and sometimes there were shouting arguments or fistfights on or near it. It was not a pleasant thing to have sitting in front of your apartment, the writer thought. At the same time, he was fascinated by almost everything that happened here.

Fact 2

It was ten or eleven o'clock when the commotion around the couch started.

The writer—who, it should be pointed out, was not *really* a writer, except in his mind (by which I mean he had not written any of the books in his head or been recognized for his craft in any substantial way)—looked out his window, through the bars, keeping his lights off so the two guys couldn't see him. They were yelling, cursing. They were familiar to the writer, but he didn't know them. The halfway they lived in was directly next door to his apartment in a line of row houses that had been built during Civil War reconstruction.

He, the writer, made a point at this time, just months after he'd moved in, just months after he had had some problems I won't bother to mention, not to talk to any of his neighbors, especially the ones from the halfway, because it was as if, he thought, their whole sad lives were contained on their faces, in their blank, sometimes angry stares as they sat on the porch bumming one another's cigarettes and whistling sarcastically at the transvestite whores.

And the writer wanted to believe, wanted to *nurture the delusion*, that he had nothing in common with these people beyond a conspicuous lack of money. When you're down, I mean *down*—when the world looks like every little promise has been lanced and bled out—you need a story to tell yourself. The young writer told himself the one about how he didn't belong here.

Assailants

One of the two assailants of the couch was a gigantic black guy—probably three hundred pounds—with an Afro that he would sometimes part in the middle, sending it out in two directions. He always wore the same hooded black sweatshirt and baggy jeans that covered most of his bright white basketball sneakers.

The other guy was thin and of Asian extraction. He wore a leather jacket with the name of a band on the back. Ether or Kepone or Nitrous, something that was just one word, chemical, punk.

Fact 3

A bottle broke, sending shards of glittering glass across the sidewalk and street, some of it hitting the van that had been parked along the curb, inert, for months. I mention this here because it was the sort of image the writer expended a great deal of energy—even, occasionally, tears—attempting to poeticize. When you cry over broken glass, it is safe to say you are not in a good mental state.

Fact Yet to Be Revealed to the Writer

The writer didn't know about his neighbor Ellis yet, who had been dead now for several hours, not even his name, or about how he'd been shot in the stomach, dropped shivering into a puddle of his own warm blood.

Gathering Info

The next day, however, the day after the night of the couch torturing, even though he was so frightened he could taste bile in the back of his throat, the writer walked up to the giant black guy as he sat on the steps of the halfway, smoking a cigarette.

The writer smiled uncomfortably, falsely, looking at the black guy's Afro. He had a big blue comb, the kind with a rounded handle that was popular in the seventies, perched atop his head, half buried in hair. The writer wondered what brought him here—schizophrenia, drugs, a minor chemical imbalance, or had he just been released from jail.

He wondered. He stared.

—You got a eye problem?

The writer said Yes, he usually wore glasses, always having had a thing for sarcasm in tense situations, particularly tense, *dangerous* situations, and for a second he waited for the black guy to get up and try to split his face open with his huge black fists. But the black guy smiled; he had a sense of humor. The writer instantly felt better.

He asked him about the couch, said that he was just wondering.

—Why the fuck you wondering? the black guy said, but it didn't sound threatening; more like: Why would anyone care?

He said he was just curious, that maybe one day, when he didn't live around here anymore, he'd want to write about it.

Smiling, the black guy offered the writer a cigarette. He turned out to be a nice guy. —A writer, he said, laughing. —Bet there's a lot of writers around here.

The writer told him he once published a story in an "avant-garde" journal he was sure nobody ever read, the kind of thing that surprises you with its existence. He told him they paid him thirty dollars. The black guy laughed.

They kept talking.

When the writer mentioned the couch again, which was just a black stain on the sidewalk now, the black guy told him his version of Ellis. Later

the writer looked in the paper. Sure enough, there
was the Ellis story—two paragraphs in the back of
the Metro section. The two versions of the story
were entirely different, though, as you might
imagine. Later the writer would think that you had
to crack open your skull and let speculation in to
understand this at all.

Anthony's Story

According to Anthony (that was the black guy's
name, Anthony, so from now on I will stop refer-
ring to him as "the black guy," which I don't *think*
is offensive, but then again, who knows), Ellis was
smoking crack. Smoking it all the time. The person who ran the halfway, a city social worker,
found a glass pipe and kicked him out. They had
a very strict policy about drugs.

Ellis, suddenly homeless, went to his ex-wife's
apartment down in the tenements (they weren't ex
officially—and Anthony took a long time to explain this part—because it cost about a thousand
dollars to get a divorce in Virginia and they didn't
have that kind of money; so they were still married
but they pretended to be divorced).

Ellis had two kids. Two boys, fairly young. His
not-really-ex-wife was pregnant again, but this one
wasn't his, which hurt, in a way, but was also a

relief. He couldn't afford the first two, much less the third.

Ellis stood in the doorway of his not-really-ex-wife's apartment, smiling, or trying to, but looking more like he was gritting his teeth to stave off some unbearable pain. His lips were blue, or purple. His eyes were yellow, red veins squiggling in every direction like secondary roads on an old map. He had no saliva. His mouth, extending down his throat to his roiling guts, was lined with fur and dust and cobwebs. He was jonesing bad, said Anthony. He acted *aggressively*, said the paper.

Ellis asked his not-really-ex-wife for money—ten bucks, five bucks, a buck. She said something to the effect of Fuck you. He hit her. Hard. He had to, really. She obviously wanted him to die. Because that's what he was doing, right now, in this dimly lit, roach- and rat-infested hallway—dying. He had often beaten his wife during the marriage (or while they lived together and were married). Ellis loved her so much it made him crazy, Anthony said, made him get high and want to kill her so other people couldn't touch her, couldn't learn her thoughts, so she couldn't go around snuffing out the last cooling embers of his heart with those high heels.

But Anthony assured the writer that she could

take it and get up swinging. She often, he said, kicked Ellis's ass. Once she stabbed him in the hip-bone with a steak knife. They used to be in love, Anthony said, really seriously in love, and sometimes, you know, that makes people want to do terrible, terrible things.

Ellis knocked her down this time. Then he went into his son's—the older one's, if the writer heard the story right—room to take stuff, money or just things he might be able to sell, quickly, to somebody on the street. Only his son, who was twelve, said Fuck you, too, you ain't my dad, and the truth is, again according to Anthony, nobody really knew if he was actually the father or not.

Ellis "freaked." Nobody respected him anymore. He'd changed this kid's diapers, sat up all night with him once when he was sick. Eyes closed, swinging wildly, he cracked open his son's—or probably his son's—face like a rotten cantaloupe. He started breaking stuff around the apartment—a radio, a picture frame, a mirror.

Then he broke the Nintendo Game Boy he had bought for his son two Christmases ago, back when he was working nights at the condom factory on the south side of Richmond, near the cigarette factories, back before the crack and the couple of short stints in county and the halfway and more crack and then the getting kicked out of the halfway and the needing crack and this sad scene in the government-housing tenements.

Ellis started crying. Bawling. He didn't want to live like this. He hated violence, really—it made him physically sick sometimes—but what else did he have, especially now, feeling like he did?

He stopped, stood still. The room, the building, the city, the spinning earth, hummed softly under his feet. His cranium was lined with wet moss. There was an itch at the center of his being that could only be scratched by a nice lungful of crack smoke (Anthony knew a lot about the specifics of crack, but the writer didn't ask how).

There was a lot of screaming in the apartment, but Ellis didn't hear it because he was standing in his own closed-off, soundproof capsule of regret, holding a smashed Nintendo Game Boy.

Ellis got it in his mind, which was not in a good state right now, to get his son—or most likely his son—who was bleeding badly, whom he was sorry for hitting, whom he loved, deep down, a Nintendo Game Boy. Tonight. A new one. He didn't have any money, of course. He'd spent it all on crack. That's why he was here, why all this commotion had just taken place, why his eyeballs were filled with sand, why his numb teeth wiggled like loose nails fastened up into his bony face, a big part of why he was crying. The circularity, the mind-bending cruelty of the whole episode, made his jaw tighten, the veins in his neck pulse.

Ellis decided to change the direction of his life, right now, by getting a Game Boy. Oh, you've heard that before—druggie decides to change his life while scraping his gaunt face against the bottom of his existence—but this is a story, or at least notes for a story, remember, even if it's true, or at the very least based on a verifiable truth, so let's give Ellis the benefit of the doubt for the next few pages. (I don't know if you believe in God, or anything God-like, but the young writer did, or wanted to, so he tried to imagine that God's light, God's beautiful beautiful light, shined, or at least *could shine*, in all of us, including himself, Ellis, and Anthony.) And let's do Anthony that favor in particular, because in truth this is mostly Anthony's story and the writer has just tried to get it all down here with a minimum of editorial intrusion.

Anthony's Theory of Tragedy

Ellis was now paranoid and superstitious and that broken Game Boy became like a voodoo doll in his hand, a palm-sized, cracked symbol of what he'd become. He had to get a new one. He picked up some of the broken stuff, set it on an old folding card table. His oldest son was on the bed, a blood-soaked pillow over his face. His wife was wailing and promising to kill him: *I'm going to kill your motherfucking ass, motherfucker!* All the neighbors in the tenement had locked their green-painted metal doors, turned up the sound on their rent-to-own TVs.

Ellis took off, left the tenements, walked and cried and thought it over. People in the writer's neighborhood (he was reading Georges Bernanos's *The Diary of a Country Priest*, which he had just found in a used bookstore, as Ellis walked under his window, so he never saw him) were actually crossing the street to avoid him, which hurt his feelings. They could sense the broken Game Boy in the front pocket of his army coat, he thought.

He started making a lot of noise now, sniffling, groaning, half talking to the low hum in the concrete he felt in the bottoms of his old, stolen shoes. A new Nintendo Game Boy was his last chance.

Ellis decided to peacefully rob—very low-key, in and out—the 7-Eleven a block from the writer's apartment and the halfway and the couch, a place the writer walked to every morning to buy coffee and a copy of the *Post* and pick up a free copy of a slim paper produced by ex-cons and current inmates, which he found fascinating, and usually to give one homeless person or another his change because it was easier than smiling and saying no, even though, technically, he needed his change.

Ellis walked into the store, browsed. He knocked over a basket of muffins by the coffee machines. He looked like a zombie in a bad late-night movie—eyes bugging out of his head, skin ashy, the corners of his lips white, pasty. The three clerks' eyes followed him, heads swinging around slowly like surveillance cameras.

The "Attack"

Ellis picked up one of those plastic knives they have by the Slurpee machine, for microwave burritos, spreading mustard on your hot dog. He waved it around threateningly.

—Empty the register, he said, but his throat was raw from smoking crack. It came out low, like a soft growl.

—What? said one clerk.

He repeated himself, which angered him, because he wanted to be the kind of person who only said things once. There were a few customers in the 7-Eleven. They didn't even stop what they were doing.

—Get out of here, the young clerk said.

There was, obviously, a metaphysical tinge to

the moment (this is how the writer would later think about this material): Ellis was fighting to save his own soul, to save his relationship with his son, or the kid who was most likely his son, to save whatever chance he still had at life. He imagined wrapping up the Game Boy in nice paper with a bow, presenting it to his son. He needed just a few tens out of the drawer. And the clerk, this guy with a goatee and nose ring, wearing a green frock, a guy who played bass badly in a local punk band, was being condescending.

Ellis took a swipe at him, gave him a small scrape on the top of his hand, the one that went, clumsily, on the neck of the bass. The clerk looked at his hand. There was a red abrasion, but no blood. He looked at Ellis and shook his head in annoyance. Then he called the cops. He put his hand over the mouthpiece of the phone and said, leering at Ellis, —This is the cops. *On the phone.*

Evidence 2

A chocolate-covered cherry, baseball cards: Ellis grabbed a chocolate-covered cherry, a few packs of baseball cards, and ran out.

The "Showdown"

The cops pulled up alongside him before he'd made it very far (the neighborhood was, for obvious reasons, heavily patrolled). They told him, through a speaker, to stop running. Anthony thought that the clerk said Ellis had a knife without specifying that it was plastic, would barely cut through a hot burrito.

Ellis wouldn't stop. He couldn't. He was on a mission. He just kept running, thinking about how he was going to buy his son a Game Boy, give him a big hug, maybe hang around, play him a game of computer football. He would do that for his son. He was going to change.

Finally, he stopped, put his hands up, and turned around. They had a spotlight on him. Trash fled up the street. Ellis couldn't see anything but white light in the direction of the cop car. It was high-volt halogen and angelic. He would just explain himself, he thought. He started walking toward the light.

He reached into the front pocket of his army jacket to pull out the broken Game Boy, evidence to the truth of his story, the importance of his mission, the essential, though perhaps damaged, goodness he knew he still had in his heart.

His throat was scorched, so as he walked quickly toward them to show them the evidence, he was mumbling, saying a lot of things that the cops couldn't understand, panicky crackhead stuff, excuses that sounded great in his mind but somehow morphed into nonsense while laid over in his dry mouth.

They told him to stop and take his hand out of his coat.

A white rookie cop, using a standard-issue .38-caliber pistol, shot him in the stomach as he started walking more quickly toward them with his hand still in his coat.

Death Scene

Ellis's coat opened and out dropped the baseball cards, the plastic knife, the chocolate-covered cherry, and the broken Nintendo Game Boy. The bullet made a clean path through his flesh and muscle and organs and ruptured the aorta, adjacent to his spine. His body cavity filled with blood, putting pressure on his lungs, impeding his breathing. He bled a polluted river of memories and regrets from his mouth. Technically speaking, he was about to suffocate.

His eyes stayed open, wobbled momentarily, as

if he was staring up into the descending asses of angels. Because angels, the writer would later think, are projections from the world, from human consciousness and imagination, they would, at this late date, as they fell from the sky for Ellis, be equipped with enormous cunts and cocks, with assholes and O-shaped mouths, would look, in fact, like AMAZINGLY LIFE-LIKE!® sex dolls with dirty wings.

Ellis died right there on the cold sidewalk, in a spreading puddle of his own warm blood, which, if anyone would have checked, had a very high content of cocaine and alcohol.

Anthony Concludes

—You're lucky to be white, Anthony said to the young writer at the end of his version of the story. —If Ellis was white, he'd be alive. I bet they would have just used a taser on you, or mace.

He was right, of course—the writer knew that if he had done the same thing he would not have been shot. Beaten and arrested, certainly, but not dead.

That was the end of Anthony's story, or rather the part of this story for which his information is mostly responsible.

We Need an Ending

But we need to continue. The writer could not take this story as it was—the hard, ridiculous facts, the two empty, antiseptic paragraphs tucked into the back of a paper. He *could not take it*. Life, he thought, is sometimes intolerable. Though he is a great despiser of the cliché, he wrote: *My heart is broken*. He felt sick. He felt the little broken heart pieces crunching around in his chest like bits of glass in a plastic bag.

So, in an effort to save this story from its hopelessness and violence and stupidity, in an effort to resuscitate some *modicum* of meaning, he turned to the couch.

The writer was intrigued even more now by the couch as an image carrying weight, as a metaphor for something, anything: rage, sorrow, something. Once he realized that the couch and Ellis were a part of the same story, that there were unseen connections all over this sad section of this Southern city, he felt as if he'd solved some utterly pointless puzzle with nothing to do but take it apart and start over again.

That was the thing about the writer—he was always mulling things over, often rather depressingly, looking for, or trying to invent, just the smallest glimmer of sense. This was selfish—but kindhearted, he liked to think—because *he* was the one in need of all the meaning. *He* was the one who needed saving.

So here comes the real ending, which is, if not happy, at least active and not passive and pointless and bloody: the night of Ellis's death, the writer was looking out his window, like I said, at these two guys, Anthony and the skinny Asian punk rocker, beating up the couch that lived in front of his apartment.

They hit it with a baseball bat. They threw bottles at it. When they sprayed it with lighter fluid and lit it on fire, the writer thought he'd better call the cops. Then he decided against it. He was new here, and he didn't want to be known as someone who called the cops.

He figured the couch was surrounded by concrete. What could happen? He watched them burn and curse the couch, as if it were evil, as if it were somehow a whole squadron of the one cop who shot Ellis, as if it had taken everything that had ever meant anything to them and destroyed it without a thought.

It was quite a blaze. Their shadows went dancing crazy up apartment building walls. And the fire department didn't show for a good half hour. In fact, the couch, that hive of disease, that beacon for fighting and illegal communing, was black springs and charred foam by the time they arrived—smoking cinders, a rectangular black stain, a writer's sad metaphor in desperate need of a story.

secret history

of home cinema

A *child* *appears* *on* *the* *screen,* grainy and out of focus, shimmering in dull pastels. It is the simplest of home movies: a child outside, in a blue plastic pool, knee-deep in water. You watch the picture get bumped onto the wall and then back onto the old vinyl screen as some cousin or brother or sister adjusts the focus, aligns the images.

You are here, in this dark and crowded living room, with your friend (soon to be your lover, but that comes later). The boy in the film is connected to your friend, whose hand you are holding—the child of your friend's divorced sister who has had her problems but is now, you heard after dinner, *straightening up, getting back on track*, etcetera. Your friend knows the history of this child, his idiosyncrasies, the fact that he wets himself still, that he speaks only in fragmentary English, that his mother's boyfriend, Robert, who set up the film and gathered the family around, drinks too much, *leads an unexamined life* and is probably the *product of abuse*, according to your friend.

You know—because of the buzz of extended-family gossip—that this child was caught in kindergarten stuffing his own feces up the bathroom spigot to make the water brown, an action that seemed, at the moment you heard about it, replete with so many dark possibilities that it was, literally, beyond reply. So you nodded, with a straight face.

Your friend warned you about the family on the way here in the car, providing a brief summary of almost everyone in the room with you now. But that kind of briefing, the let-me-warn-you-about-my-family kind, is always either downplayed or exaggerated, placing the truth somewhere in between extremes.

You sip your drink as Robert appears onscreen with the child, and you wonder who's holding the camera. The mother? The child, the real child as opposed to his image onscreen, is sleeping in the grandmother's bedroom with his mother who had a headache. Robert, the flesh-and-blood Robert, is telling you how 16 mm film is superior to video, how it still has the possibilities of art contained in its makeup, although not much commercial viability. He says how he was going to go to film school until he *realized you have to eat, ha ha.* And you thank God for capitalism (clearly, you smile, the true philosophy of God).

[*cut to: thumb, grass, water* . . .]

The child bounces in the pool, orange floats with duck heads surround his biceps, his small stomach distended in the way of young children not yet programmed to suck in their guts, like everyone in the room is doing after the large meal.

The cousin or brother or sister turns up the sound. You haven't connected names to faces yet, and you're a little drunk and it's too dark to see anyway. The audio sputters in sync with the shifting images. Lines resembling insects appear and vanish.

The camera is a remarkable thing, you think, with its ability to transform the mundane into an immortal moment able to travel through time, reappear days or months or years after its actual occurrence. Every second of our existence is alive with possibility, but we don't see it until we hit rewind, until we freeze the frame. It is sad that so many things, all suffused with meaning, escape the unaided eye.

[*cut to: darkness, bare feet, a baseball field, the child in a hat too big for his head . . .*]

—Okay, hit the ball. Give it a good one, says Robert from out of camera range, his voice slightly higher through the filter of the machine.

The angles are crude, amateurish—wide pans, pointless close-ups, the field tilting like an airplane wing. There is no craft at work here, no politic or sociology, no aesthetics: it's random, accidental, honest.

—It hurts, says the child. —Don't want to. He is looking at the ground, hugging himself with one arm as he chews, actually *chews*, on his other hand. The bat is at his feet.

—Pick up the bat and hit the ball, says Robert. —The film's rolling. Do you want the whole world to see you acting like a retard? Just think, millions of people out there in TV land seeing how much of a baby you are, how you won't even try to hit a baseball.

You turn your head, glancing at your friend, the person who brought you here, deeper inside these strangers' lives than you want to be. Your friend is drinking an imported beer—a particularly fashionable imported beer recently promoted by a clever ad campaign—leaning back, seemingly bored by the flickering images.

[*cut to: trees, sky, ground, feet . . .*]

48

The boy is holding the bat now, pathetically, you think, letting it hang over the back of his shoulder.

—All right all right all right, boy, knock this thing into outer space, to the next planet. Ready?

—It hurts. The child chews his hand again, looking away from the voice and the camera, as if he were averting his eyes from you. The bat slips from his hand and hits the ground. He begins crying, silently, or at least not loud enough to be captured on audio.

—Pick up the bat, retard, says Robert. —Your mom's going to see this. She'll know that you can't even have fun without crying.

Your friend is calm beside you, slowly sipping the beer. The same person who fascinated you by being so aware only hours ago. The person who talks endlessly about progressive politics, who rambles on about French deconstruction and friends' dissertations and David Cronenberg's sexualizing of technological gadgetry and the pre-postmodern self-effacing irony of Chaplin and Shepard's dialogue in *Paris, Texas* and how that film was *really about human suffering, you know*; the person who talks about writing a book about you can't remember what, but it seemed deep at the time you first heard it, at the end of your first-date/get-to-know-each-other/casual thing, as the two of you smoked

a joint and later had your first kiss and thought of
making love but didn't because you wanted it to
be special, meaning semi-sober, and later, after a
nice dinner and conversation and maybe discussion of the greater philosophical questions concerning love and the soul and whether people
actually had *soul mates*, which made you laugh a
little, even though secretly you were hopeful,
wanting more than anything an easy human con-
nection, love, or something like love, without all
the fucking work. This same friend, this soon-to-
be lover, is motionless and stone-faced as the child
cries on the screen.

Robert, leaning toward you in confidence and,
you assume, a gesture of camaraderie, says how the
kid is a basket case, how his father, whom Robert
calls an asshole, just took off and left the kid and
his mother. Just like that. He tells you how the kid
needs discipline and hard lessons, how the kid will
adjust to a strict, yet loving, environment and be
a better person for it. He tells you how he had to
do something because the mother, your friend's
sister, whom you met earlier at dinner while both
of you hit the wine a little too hard, just couldn't
handle him anymore with the copro . . . copra . . .
corpa . . . playing-with-shit stuff.

You feel his breath in your ear as the child
chews his hand on the screen.

[*cut to: child, smiling, at home plate, holding the bat over his shoulder . . .*]

—Okay, buddy, that was good. Good hit. But hold on to the bat like I showed you, says Robert, who must have been holding the camera to his eye as he pitched because of the soft, swaying movement of the image, the ball appearing from the bottom of the screen.

The child repositions the bat and drops it. He stares down at the bat, then covers his face, as if this were the worst failure one might ever know in life. And this reminds you of all the failing you've done. Even a successful life, like yours, could be charted by connecting the endless stream of failures. It might look like a nautical map, with deep blue showing the bigger losses and humiliations.

—Ate you, says the image of the child. *I hate you*, you decipher, *I hate you.*

For an instant, the camera moves into close-up, you think, but then you realize Robert is walking toward the boy.

—Pick up the bat, he says.

The boy begins running. He trips. The camera keeps shooting.

[*cut to: feet, legs, feet, dirt . . .*]

—Look, I haven't got time for this. Pick up the bat . . .

[*cut to: black*]

You consider the tone of Robert's last statement. It wasn't malicious, exactly, or even menacing, but really just exasperated—a man fed up with the pressures of a difficult child.

Your friend takes this break as an opportunity to escape, which the two of you will joke about later, and says that you've got to get going, actually, that the two of you have quite a long drive back to the city. And that's all your friend says. No outrage. No minor activism. No deep reading of the film or discussion of how the blunt images seemed, to you at least, nearly pornographic.

If it were *my* family, you think . . .

And here begins the breakup of the relationship you haven't even begun. In the film of the child. In yourself. In the coldness you now suspect in your friend.

The two of you will fight in the car on the way back to the city and it will be your first fight (you haven't even disagreed yet), and later you will make love for the first time. And the lovemaking will be very good because of the energy produced from the anger and verbally inflicted injuries, which will still be reverberating in the air like an echo. This first lovemaking will also contain the element of regret and the intent of healing with soft touches and flesh against flesh—which will corroborate your notion that you're normal.

But first comes the fight. In the car, you won't mention the film. It will seem too sad and sick and dangerous, too obvious, to even bring up. So the fight will be under the guise of jealousy. It will pertain to something about an ex-lover who keeps turning up in all the right or wrong places (depending on perspective) around the city—restaurants, bookstores, bars, coffeehouses—precisely when the two of you go to these places. The fight tonight in the car on the way back to the city will get nasty and personal, but it won't be nearly as bad as the fights you will have later. Those will get ugly.

The later fights will get ugly because the two of you will know that the end is coming, and with every insult, every long cold silence and refusal to touch, will be the attitude of let's just get it over with, the understanding that cruelty might speed up the process. (It will.) But even then there will be a part of you that feels compelled to hold on, that will remember all the physical and mental and emotional investments that connect the two of you.

And sex, of course, will be the hardest of these investments to finally give up. Because despite everything that's coming, the sex will, for the most part, be good on a bad day and toe-curling, wake-up-the-neighbors great on a good day. Sex. The mere mention of the word will arouse you. And this wonderful and sad fucking will exacerbate the pain (but in a way that is not entirely negative).

However, things will be great, for a while, as they usually are in something worth calling a relationship. And you will tell people, lots of people, how great things are, which will make the end, the explaining and reexplaining of why it didn't work, even more depressing and humiliating.

But first, not far from the now of this story, during the great time, you will invest yourself completely, give yourself over to this lover's fantasies with unencumbered trust. And vice versa. And one of these fantasies—not yours—will involve a palm-sized camcorder, a distant relative of the 16 mm camera that Robert is packing up now. You will always worry about the videotape of the two of you appearing somewhere, tangled together and grunting in a way you will find unsettling, actually kind of sad and wonderful like those last parting fucks will be. The audio of the tape will be filled with your moaning and expletives and commands and you'll think: *Damn, do I sound like that? I don't sound like that.*

You will imagine yourself naked on television

screens in hospital waiting rooms and up in the corners of bars as tattooed men ogle you and joke about a blemish on your ass. Your heart will speed up when you see coin-operated TVs in bus stations and when you think of the small, blue screens hanging from the ceiling in the business-class section of an airplane. You will actually have a dream about watching yourself awkwardly fucking (performing a sort of anti-porn) on a wall of a thousand televisions in the back of a Circuit City.

But all of this is much, much later.

Right now you are still trying to get out of your friend's family's house. Everyone is standing up, following the two of you toward the door, patting you on the back and saying how nice it was to meet you and that they hope you will come back and visit. And you will come back and visit because your relationship with your friend—which will begin just hours from now when you put your hand on the soft inner part of your friend's leg and say you're sorry and then make a self-deprecating joke as a prelude to the kiss that will *get things rolling*—will last for almost two years, if you count the last few months as on as opposed to off, which will be up for debate.

You stand at the door after shaking hands and want desperately to say something about the film of the child, even though there is no evidence with which to accuse anyone of anything, just vague, poorly captured images and a sinking feeling. You want your friend to say something, to stand up for the child, because your friend, when you get right down to it, is a bit smarter than you and a lot more articulate and able to point out not only the problem as it manifests itself in reality but also its *deeper causes*.

To break the uncomfortable silence, you say it was nice meeting everyone. Another long silence, empty looks, head-nodding, frozen smiles.

That's it. You smile back. And you hate your smile. You are flooded with the vague energy of disgust, which you will sweat out later tonight as you bump knees and noses trying to *find a groove*.

Your soon-to-be lover already seems distant to you—before anything even happens, before you have even given each other pet names—like a negative of the person you've been wanting. You won't think of this moment as significant later, at the end. There will have been too many moments to consider by then, all containing their own amount of clarity and confusion, cause and effect. There will be no record, no rewind, no freeze-frame. It will vanish from your consciousness like a shadow in direct light, like a spent reel of film.

The family is smiling and waving. You are turning and walking down the driveway toward the car, holding your soon-to-be-lover's hand. The future spreads out in front of you. Streetlights hum. The night is black and cold. You stare ahead through your own breath.

1967

he himself grows in me we eat our defeats
we burst out laughing
when they say how little is needed
to be reconciled
    —Zbigniew Herbert, "Remembering My Father"

*H*ere is how I imagine it, how I
might begin the book of my father, with
a vision of his mother, under a mottled Virginia
sky that promises rain, gray rolling over bruise-
colored gray, faint streaks of yellow from the sun
like a healing outer edge. Their dilapidated house
on a street of dilapidated houses, all built in the
thirties, during the Depression, when, as the rest
of the country suffered, southeast Virginia grew fat
and strong around a shipbuilding industry and military bases—the fear of fascism and communism in
Europe. A single chicken pecks hungrily in the
overgrown yard. It is 1967. The old house, like

every house on this short side street, has long since forgotten what prosperity was like: wind whips through its seams; the roof sags like the spine of an aged horse. And a woman, old beyond her years, sits under the cracked and splintered porch eaves, dressed in a dirty pink nightgown, a single pale, sagging breast hanging lifelessly out of the material. She is drinking the heart out of a darkening fall afternoon. A group of young boys on bikes laugh, in the vacant street, never taking their eyes from the pink, misshapen nipple. It sparkles like a coin to them. Occasionally these boys shoot BB guns at the woman from the woods. Because children are innocent and cruel. Because they haven't thought much about her—except to ponder her misshapen breasts. She is a subhuman redneck. She swats the BBs as if they are mosquitoes, gets a swatter to hold in her lap while she drinks, puts calamine lotion over the welts that, oddly, don't itch. *Go to hell*, she would shout in this opening scene, taking a drink.

My father pulls his '65 Mustang, the best thing he has ever owned, into his mother's pocked driveway. It is three years before he is my father and twenty-six years before his funeral, where a great-uncle I barely know, almost weep-ing, gives me this story, the one that could serve as the beginning of a book, if I only had the patience and the strength, the memory and the nerve; it was, as he told it, a broken story in need of great repair, but also a good one, or so it seemed to me, one that still trails me around. It was a backward story, the way he told it, an anti-tragedy, one that began with death and ended with life—a wishful story at a time when wishing seemed futile. And in this story, as it was told to me and as I might reimagine it, my father stands in the overgrown yard, staring at the boys in the street, making eye contact with the leader, giving his meanest look, which, I remember, was fairly tepid. The kids, like kids, ride off, shouting, *Your mom has nice tits!*

He is medium-build, my father, in 1967, with dark blue eyes and freckles. He is Scotch Irish. His hair is reddish brown and wavy, fashionably unkempt, and long, bushy sideburns reach past his earlobes. He's wearing *brown velour.* He likes Creedence Clearwater Revival and The Who. He is unconventionally handsome, I think, in the few pictures I still have of him. He looks at his mother, his eyes moving immediately to her sagging breast, white as a new golf ball. Jesus, he thinks, not as prayer but as lament. His father, her husband, has recently died, at the age of fifty, of a heart attack, and his mother, who has been drinking like this for years, has now been drunk for several straight weeks. Soon she will wreck a new car bought with insurance money; later, before she is put into a psychiatric ward, she will catch the house on fire by letting a cigarette fall from her whisky-wet lips.

My father and his father barely spoke, just as my father and I, at times, will barely speak. My father loved his father, though, in a quiet, obligatory way. They never hugged, generally kept their distance, but they would have fought for each other, broken a pool cue over someone's head for each other. It was that kind of love. He made his father's funeral arrangements, spent all his money on the service, and still, as of fall 1967, owes some.

Something about my father's father: When my father decided he would return to high school after dropping out for two years, the old man resented him, called him "uppity." He made fun of high school, talked of the righteousness of hard work with your hands and your back. He had been a migrant farmer as a boy, had worked hard and long, then spent years as a laborer, going where the work was, until he quit all of that toward the end of his life for some ill-advised moneymaking ventures: a flop of a grocery store in a bad part of town, a pig farm that put them deep into debt. On my father's graduation day, 1962, as students two years younger than he huddled with their families for pictures and sang songs and then went off to celebrate, my father walked sullenly to a friend's house, where several high-school dropouts sat around drinking beer and watching baseball on an old TV. During the ceremony—the speeches and congratulations—my father's father was sitting on a bench in front of the gas station, staring at the traffic; his mother was passed out in her bedroom. That night my father got drunk and never mentioned the ceremony, which was, after all, just a ceremony.

Now, in this story, the one the great-uncle told me, my father walks up the drive toward the small house. His mother sees him but says nothing. He loves his mother, too, but the love feels like an obligation, sometimes a curse. It is an exhausting sort of love. He thinks, and will always think until his death, that love is often more work than it deserves. He has come out here several times this month, to find her sleeping in the woods, sleeping with the oven on, sleeping in a neighbor's front yard at night with the group of boys around her, laughing. He imagined the boys pissing on her and chased them. He imagined the urine dripping off her forehead, her eyelashes, as she smiled in a dead sleep. To the neighbors, the scene must have been both sad and comical: the neighborhood drunk slumped half dead in the yard, her half-crazy son chasing the boys again. The western sky, he notices, is the color of the veins in her legs. Her circulation is poor. Her blood is thinned by alcohol, her heart pumps slowly. Mr. Purcell, a neighbor, a kind old pipe fitter for NASA, called about the stink: *I reckon a coon or a big old black snake got up under the house and died. It smells something awful over there.* The phone call alarmed my father. He remembered the last call about the smell.

Sometimes my father dreams of his father, as I will dream of my father. Dreams are like the best books, I sometimes think: they tell you things you may not want to hear; they challenge you to think something, feel something; they make you uncomfortable, because every dream, no matter what it is about, is about the dreamer. In dreams, my father pushes his father's head down a hole in the street; his father shoots his mother for wildly fucking another man while drunk; his father gargles soup at the rusty-legged, linoleum-topped kitchen table—that's it, just leans his head back and audibly, almost musically, gargles soup; my father finds himself along the shores of the Chesapeake Bay, walking the beach, searching for his father's eyes like fiddler crabs so he can put his father back together—everything depends on finding his father's eyes, which are nowhere to be found.

He is here, again, for the stink.

Something else that should go into this book I'm not going to write: Once, not long before his death, my father's father drove my father's old car off of a bridge. The bridge was new. You could look through police records and see that he was the first person to get a car to go off that bridge. People scratched their heads over this; it pointed out a design flaw. Cars weren't supposed to just go sailing into the bay. A sailor from Norfolk—this is true—jumped off the bridge and saved him. It was in the paper. It was like something from a movie—if you focused on the heroism of the sailor rather than all the complicated stuff about the victim. The logical question is: Did he try to commit suicide or was this simply an accident? It's unclear. The answers are lost to history. But he never thanked the sailor. And he never apologized to my father for crashing his car, which, as far as I know, is still on the sandy bottom of the bay.

About that earlier scene: My father tucks his mother's breast in and she pays no attention. It is oddly cold in his hand. Her face is gaunt, collapsing, eyes yellow as a healthy boy's urine. But she remarks with lucidity about the weather as she stares out at the thick, wet distance, says how it will be too rough to fish later, as if it were possible for her to fish later without doing her own falling off of bridges. So he would sit on the bench beside his mother, surely he would do this, put his head in his hands, sigh—a practiced gesture.

His mother and father were separated at the time of his father's death. She was in the hospital having a procedure done for an ulcer (they performed surgery on them back then). My father got a call from the cops. They had found his father three days after he'd died from a massive heart attack. My father had to go to the house, sign some papers, answer some questions, identify, verify. It was still hot then. You can imagine. The body was swollen. The skin was gray. Eyes open. It was as if he'd drowned, a delayed reaction to driving off the bridge. Maybe he'd been dead for a long time, my father might have thought, and had waited to lie down in darkness and start stinking to let everyone know. His dog, Henry, a terrier mutt, was lying still beside the body, ready to go out. Henry had been hiding under the bed when the cops came in earlier. The dog perked up its ears, wagged its tail when my father opened the door. My father ejected sickness and disbelief into his open hands, instinctively trying to avoid making a mess in his father's house.

Something about my father's mother: My father had a pet rabbit as a boy, a little white one named Bugs, and one day his mother told him to go get it. She was sober. He handed it to her with complete trust. He was maybe ten, eleven, not yet cynical, wary. He knew nothing of alcoholism, madness, suicide. All of that was later, still too early for a boy, but later. She broke the rabbit's neck with her bare hands. It screamed. Rabbits can scream like wounded babies. When he cried and refused to eat Bugs, his father said, Fine, more for me. On this fall day in 1967, he thinks of this when the smell hits him, even, oddly, before he thinks of his father's swollen, gray body. He can't believe she could sit here, no matter how drunk, in this smell.

She keeps drinking and talking of fishing, of blue skies, of the time they went, just the two of them, right after they were married, down to Florida, to the Gulf Coast. Blue water and huge colorful fish. These words could be anything: baby talk, the grocery list, another fishing story. She is unraveling, tiptoeing toward psychotic breakdown. She doesn't look at my father. She goes on. He (my father's father) caught one so big that they grilled it and fed everyone at the hotel. They were heroes for a day. They smoked cigars in the sun. They were wearing new clothes. They both had jobs back in Virginia. It was a beautiful day. They had coleslaw and French fries and big hunks of exotic fish. Her nightgown opens again. She doesn't notice, or simply doesn't care, he can't tell. She tries to conjure other good days, furrows her brow at the chicken pecking in the yard. She drinks from a tall, chipped tea glass. My father walks into the house to get a flashlight so that he can get under the house and see what's dead. He takes a bandana from his pocket, one of those red paisley ones, and puts it over his face, tying it behind his head like Billy the Kid. He feels like a boy.

The smell of death sends him reeling, thinking of the rabbit, his father's swollen body. The luck of this house. He had aspirations of playing major-league baseball, of living far from all this. He'd gone out West with the national championship all-star baseball team from Virginia, 1960, and the sky, just like he'd heard, was enormous, limitless, not like in the South, where it was low and wet all the time, even when it was sunny, reminding you always of the boundaries of your life. The West— Montana, Colorado, Utah—that space, that vast American emptiness, made his heart grow big in his chest, made his scalp tingle with possibility. Growing up he sometimes felt like a speck on the sad, wet earth. The shouting and the drinking and the occasional tossing of dishes had closed in on him like walls. Instead of getting tough, he became overly sensitive, moody, lacking confidence in everything from school to girls, everything but his ability to hit and field a ball. And then he ruined his knee, just kidding around with dropouts, playing basketball in a pair of slippery loafers. (Dreams are so fragile that they can be taken away by a pair of slippery loafers.) The injury kept him out of Vietnam, sure, but it also kept him out of baseball; it kept him away from what he imagined was his only chance to live out in the open, free, to live a life that was not obscene.

But he did find ways. He kept his head above water; he didn't go driving off of a bridge.

He rifles through drawers, looking for the flashlight. We are back in the opening scene of the imaginary book. The smell is strong, maybe too strong to be under the house. He can't find the flashlight. After hurting his knee, after the doctors told him it would never be right again, my father was depressed. He was stuck in his life as it was. He ran his father's grocery store after dropping out of school. It was when the store went under that he returned to school and graduated. Then he took care of his father's pig farm, something his father bought before he died, thinking it would make money. It didn't. He sold all the pigs to slaughter after his father's death—for a loss, but good riddance. Soon he would work in a bank. Then, finally, by 1970, the year I was born, he'd take a job

at the Newport News Shipyard, this when he'd
conceded that he would never fulfill his dreams
and that he needed to imagine new things to
dream.

But on this particular day, he is unemployed.

It's not under the house. It's Henry, my
father's father's dog. That's the big twist, the
O. Henry moment in imaginary chapter one. Dead
in the bedroom, on the bed. Dead for a while, a
few days. Jesus, he thinks, not as prayer but as lament, what is it with this? How do these things
go unnoticed? The dog is collapsed. Dead for a
week or more. He thinks Henry may have starved,
barked and whined and panicked until he finally
lay down to sleep, but then pushes the thought
away. Heart attack. Old age. Easier. Neater. He
picks up Henry and thinks of the rabbit, his father,
and now his mother out on the porch and those
boys who go in the woods to shoot BBs at her,
who stand around her when she's drunk and dare
each other. If he were not himself, he thinks, holding the stinking dog, and he were instead one of
those boys, one of those boys with their whole

futures in front of them to ruin, he'd probably do the same thing. He imagines shooting BBs at his mother, standing over her in the yard, in the dark, daring himself and the boys to degrade her.

Here is how bad my father's luck—and by genealogical extension my own luck, my family's luck—was. He eventually died, almost twenty-six years to the day from the dog incident, of malignant mesothelioma caused by asbestos fibers, which he got while working for more than two decades at the Newport News Shipyard. That may seem too lachrymose, too contrived, to even put in a book. When I think of this, his illness, I think of baseball, of his knee, of dead rabbits and dogs and fathers, of dreams and dead dreams and dreams of death as ordered and uncomfortable as a good book, of the fact that his father and mother wouldn't take one fucking afternoon, a couple of hours, to go stand in a crowd for what was perhaps a pointless ceremony, a ridiculous American ritual, while my father graduated from high school at almost twenty years old (only slightly older than I was when I received a bachelor's degree, for which my father went out and spent more money than he should have on a camcorder to capture my pointless ceremony, which he made sure I knew was anything but pointless), which was one of the most difficult things he ever accomplished, which is why I'm writing these notes without the words "grandmother" and "grandfather."

Something about me, the narrator, the non–book writer: In college, for a time, I read Eastern philosophy (I might have grown a goatee if my face would have cooperated). Then I read Hesse and Kerouac and Huxley and D. H. Lawrence's ramblings from Italy and Taos, New Mexico. All that unencumbered ranting. All that love and suffering. Those books were about me. I wanted to be that sad happy tragicomic narrator bleeding that jazzy blues-filled bebop prose, a dirty reefer-stoked martyr for the lost and the fucked up and the never-quite-made-its who considered myself no more or less important than anyone or anything else. One can incorporate, attribute, luck to the karmic wheel, to *samsara*, the endless cycle of birth, suffering, death, rebirth. To yin and yang, to universal equanimity, to positive and negative sharing equal space, etcetera. Nothing has to *mean*, it just is. One can have a clean mind and body and a stoic understanding of tragedy, if trained properly, if ascetic. But I failed in every way. I am about as capable of following religious dogma as a dead mutt (dead for a week, let's say, starved to death by its drunken owner) is of winning the blue ribbon in a dog show. I took drugs and drank and drank and drank. The closest I came to stoicism was floating around in a haze, narcotized, troubled but numb.

After college, I moved to Richmond, a couple of hours up the James River from where I was born. My father was dying. I tried not to think about it; it became all I thought about. I had four jobs that year and quit them all. I fancied myself some kind of poet—part Robert Lowell, part John Berryman. I was filled with what I thought of as the necessary angst and turmoil; I was willing, in that Judeo-Christian way, to confess; I just lacked talent. I read all the time. I wanted the Western fucking canon to save me. I drank all the time. I wanted hops and barley to save me. I was frightened of my father's death as if it were my own. I rarely went home to see him, to stare into my own face, instead calling him, having incredibly positive, superficial conversations while he had trouble breathing. Distance, I hoped, would alleviate the obligation of love. It didn't, like I knew it wouldn't, like he knew it wouldn't. I was a coward. On the morning of the day my father would die, my younger brother called. He was sixteen and stayed home with my father, getting him to the bathroom, wiping his mouth. He was crying. He couldn't even talk, but I knew. I was broke. Like my father, like my grandfather, money eluded me; it seemed I wasn't supposed to have it. I didn't have money for gas to get home. I took quarters out of a jar in my roommate's room. All the signs along the highway were blank and I floated unmoored through timeless space without touching the accelerator or the steering wheel or hearing the radio that was on full volume. Two hours later, when I reached my house, there was a sign that said OXYGEN IN USE: NO SMOKING. I was stuck. I didn't want to go in. I thought, for just a second, about leaving. Inside, my father was in bed. The cancer had spread to his liver; his poisoned blood was recycling itself and pumping through his body. He was wearing a diaper. He weighed eighty pounds, having lost half his body weight in less than a year, a third of that in the month since I'd seen him. I barely recognized him. He was fifty-one. I was twenty-two. I've erased a lot of it. I remember lying in the bed with him, both of us staring at the rough, white ceiling, still shy about showing affection, even then. I don't remember what was said, but he seemed to be listening, his legs slowly writhing like things under water. Less than two hours after I'd returned home, he died. I'd swear he waited for me, that he insisted on doing me that favor. My mother, my younger brother, and I stayed in the room with him. We lay in the bed with him. Had it been my choice, at that moment, I might have washed him and kept him for three more days.

But about the dog and my father's mother, about the *dramatic action* of this story: The old great-uncle from North Carolina—a "public school administrator and a good, God-fearing man"—back at my family's house, the two of us drinking, eating ridiculously small biscuits from a tray. He finished the story. He wasn't a good story-teller. He backtracked, said, No, wait, said, And then. He let the story veer all over the place, let the action stop dead in spots for some familial or historical commentary. Then he'd pick it back up only to do it again. It was a story and a history and a confessional and an elegy and a complaint and a prayer. You might say *he tossed form out the window and laid it all out there.* My father's mother had had a psychotic breakdown. She went into a hospital that year and saw her dead brother's face in a large plant. She told the plant how her "nerves was bad" and how much she missed him, how she was alone

now and her heart was dying. Then she got better,
not great, but better. She couldn't touch booze
ever again. The couple of times she did were dis-
astrous. And my father, said the great-uncle, that
dark fall day in 1967, walked out the back door,
the stinking dead dog in his arms, the bandana over
his face, to avoid having his fragile mother see.
And that was a part of it. The point. The message,
the moral. He wanted me to understand the kindness in that gesture. She was still talking to the
chicken in the overgrown yard. The boys were in
the street, on their bikes, drinking sodas, eating
candy. My father buried Henry in the woods, dig-
ging the hole with his bare hands. That was it. End
of story. We swigged Budweiser from red, white,
and blue cans. We were getting drunk, and I'd
decided to stay drunk for as long as physically possible. Do you see, his watery eyes said, your father
was a good man.

After the funeral and the reception (or
whatever you call the non-party after funerals),
after everyone had left, and my family was asleep,
I was still drinking under a single lamp in the otherwise dark house, thinking about the story, pic-
turing my father in 1967, thinking that he looked
a little like George Jones back then, a little like

John Fogerty. I was mulling it over, storing it up. The story connected to other stories, stretching back through time, springing forward through my life, my future, even far beyond me, until I was nothing but a character in someone's story, but in that way, like my father, maybe I will never vanish, maybe I will never die.

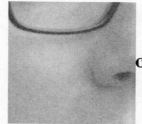 a seat for the

coming savior

i.

*S*t. James didn't think of himself as an artist. His intentions went far beyond art. He didn't think of himself as a "folk" or an "outsider" or a "grass roots" or a "visionary" artist. He didn't consider himself any of the things scholars have called him since his death in 1964. He didn't even know what those names meant, not in the way they used them, anyway. "Folk"? That's what he called his people down in Elloree, South Carolina, where his sister sat on a splintered porch thanking Jesus for the daylight, where the farmland stretched right out to the hem of the sky, where "The Best Pork Bar-B-Que in the World" was made out behind the Stop-'n'-Go. And "outsider"? Man, that one was easy: every nigger in America.

When he began *The Throne of the Third Heaven of the Nations Millennium General Assembly*, a 180-piece sculpture made from the refuse of a dying world, in that old rented garage in northwest Washington, D.C., where poverty could beat your soul into some new shape, where a man might rather put a bullet in you than shake your hand, he never would have imagined that one day it would be displayed in a museum, under fancy lighting, against a backdrop of majestic purple, where a janitor—a janitor just like him—would come by at night to dust it.

He built *The Throne* to prepare the world for the End Time, the Second Coming of Jesus Christ, our Savior, as prophesied in Revelation. He worked nights in various government buildings in the District, mopping floors and singing hymns from his childhood in Elloree, where he first saw the face of God when he was just a boy—not a shadow falling down in a corner or something smoldering at the edge of vision, not a feeling tickling in his spine or cloaking him in the Spirit's heat, but the *real face of God*—shining there in front of him one night like an explosion on a drive-in movie screen. It was at that moment that he knew he was chosen, knew he was a saint, knew that he had been granted life, this terrible, beautiful life, to serve God.

ii.

James Hampton, Jr., arrived in his family's shack in Elloree in 1909, slick and shiny with birth, face aimed skyward, screaming like a true Southern Baptist. He was named after his father, a gospel singer and self-proclaimed Baptist preacher who would later abandon his family (a wife and four children, including James) in the early 1920s to travel through the rural South and preach.

In 1928, at the age of nineteen, after a childhood of farmwork and family and strict religion, James moved to Washington, D.C., to join his older brother, Lee. The city was a new world—bigger, yet somehow claustrophobic, harsher, but beautiful, too—with the great monuments of America rising up into the sky, almost as if they somehow grew right out of the ghetto James and his brother lived in.

For more than a decade, James worked as a short-orderok in various diners around the city, keeping to himself, hearing faint voices, taking prayer breaks instead of smoke breaks when he took a break at all. At the end of a twelve-, fourteen- hour day, he walked home, slope-backed and exhausted; past men sleeping in alleys and boys hanging out on corners like packs of young wolves; past prostitutes saying, *Hey, little man, hey, Jesus, what I got make you see angels, baby.* He kept his eyes aimed at the ground—cigarettes, bottle caps, a bullet.

He wore his day home with him in a cloud of stink: old vegetables, coffee, meat, grease, garbage. And he could still hear the echoes of clanking dishes and order bells, even in the half-still city night, and somewhere down below, all the noise of the world ringing in his head—always ringing in his head—he heard the faint mutterings of God like his own teeth grinding, like his own pulse. He'd shower in the apartment he and Lee shared, read his favorite passages from the Bible—Genesis, the Gospel of John, and Revelation—and sleep the sleep made of hard work. Then he'd get up and do it all over again. Day after day. Month after month. Year after year. The noisy world in his head. And underneath the noise, just underneath it, God.

iii.

In early 1942, everything changed. James was drafted. He knew it was coming as soon he heard about Pearl Harbor on the night of December 7,

1941, right while he was squeezing the grease out of a pink, sizzling burger. Nigger like him, healthy and living in a part of the city white people didn't even drive through, he knew. But it was okay, too, a part of God's plan for him. He was a supplicant in the palm of the Father. He was thirty-three now, the same age as Jesus when they nailed him up in sunlight, and he was ready to sacrifice himself if that's what God wanted.

From 1942 to 1945, James served in the army's noncombatant 385th Aviation Squadron in Texas, and later in Seattle, Hawaii, Saipan, and Guam. His unit specialized in carpentry and maintenance, and James made (critics speculate) his first piece of *The Throne*, a small, winged object ornately decorated with foil, in 1945 on the island of Guam. He returned to Washington in 1946, after receiving a Bronze Star Medal and an honorable discharge. He rented a room in a boarding house not far from his brother's apartment. Then he found work with the General Services Administration as a janitor— not good work, but better than he would have gotten without that Bronze Star Medal and veteran status.

After a brief illness, his brother Lee died suddenly in 1948. He went to work one day feeling a little down, a bad taste in his mouth and sweat breaking out all over him—he hadn't been to a doctor in years because who could afford a doctor?—then came home, went to sleep, and never opened his eyes. They must have buried Lee down in Elloree on a bright, sunny Saturday, James reading a stitched-together elegy made of Bible passages over the grave, tears rolling down his face; the whole town gathered around, dressed up black as crows, softly singing hymns. But it was a short visit. After mourning and celebrating the ascendant soul of Lee for a day or two, James got on a train and headed back to Washington, sitting in the rear car, the "black" car, the Southern countryside smearing by his window. Lee wasn't simply James's brother, he was his best friend, maybe his only friend, and now James, alone but not lonely because he knew all things were a part of His plan, began spending all his time envisioning *The Throne*. Lee and his janitorial job were his only anchors to this world. Now Lee was gone.

Back in Washington, he went out only to work, find materials for *The Throne*, and attend a number of different churches in the city (he didn't believe God would allow for strict denominations and divisiveness concerning His word).

By 1949, at the age of forty, he felt the power of God buzzing electrically up his spine. The End Time was coming. He had sensed it during the war, in the stories he heard about what men were capable of doing to one another; he could see it now in the hard faces that hovered along sidewalks, could watch it growing in the people like a malignancy. It was both a curse and a blessing that he sensed it so acutely, felt the world's decay as a dull ache in his bones.

Some days now the low, gray sky would fill up his skull like cotton and he'd forget everything but God, forget who and where he was, and it was beautiful, this kind of forgetting, but then he'd come to on the street, walking stiff as always, General Services Administration uniform tight and clean around his small frame, and he suddenly had this *clarity*, he could see despair like a blanket of living, breathing fog over the streets. It was all he could do not to crumble as he headed to work those days, where he cleaned the floors and toilets of the people who ruled the world.

iv.

In 1950, answering the request God had made in a dream, he rented an abandoned garage at 1133 N Street NW from a local merchant, telling him he was working on something that required more space than he had. The garage was down an alley, out of sight from passersby, on a block more dangerous even than his own. It was dark and dusty, with brick walls, concrete floor, and lightbulbs dangling from wires that traveled along creaky ceiling support beams. Rats scurried in the alley, darting between Dumpsters. Spider webs formed misty veils over corners. It was awful. It was perfect. It was exactly where God wanted *The Throne* to be.

Over the next fourteen years, James found a routine. He worked until midnight, mopping floors and picking up trash in government buildings, then went to the garage to do his real work for five or six hours, listening closely to what God was telling him, finally going home to sleep when the first pink light of dawn started creeping up the Washington Monument.

Some afternoons and many weekends, he would visit local used furniture stores, rubbing his hand across coffee tables, feeling how sturdy the leg of a chair was, staring for long minutes at a rickety old chest, then asking about prices in a voice just above a whisper. If he liked something, he'd return later with a child's wagon and a pocketful of folded-over dollar bills soft and worn as tissue paper. He carted away things that had the merchants scratching their heads: legless tables, drawerless desks, half-crushed dollhouses, leaning stools.

Later, you might have seen him walking from a government building with a trash bag full of used lightbulbs; or maybe out on the street with a croaker sack, asking bums if he could buy the foil off of their wine bottles. He'd dig through Dumpsters to get green glass, sandwich foil, cardboard. And of course the best thing about working for the American government was how wasteful they were, throwing out perfectly good material because they didn't like the way it looked. Sometimes he'd even get brand-new stuff because someone ordered twice what was actually needed. It made him smile, these finds. The best thing about cleaning up after the people who ruled the world was that they didn't see the real value in things.

v.

Occasionally, after long hours of work, after a face full of government cleaning chemicals and toxic solvents, his brains felt like Jell-O bumping up against his skull, and bits of time disappeared like old pennies. But other days everything was sharp and sensible. On these days of clarity, James . . . *Saint* James turned into God's lightning rod, a cipher for the Word.

He had grown up with the Bible. Bible was his first language. He could remember his father preaching in Elloree, sweat on his forehead like a field of blisters, people standing around in the backyard *testifying*. *Praise God!* He knew the power of God before he had any inkling of Self, knew later that there was no worthy Self without Him. But when he had these days of clarity, of *vision*, that's when he knew the world was ignoring God and His commandments, knew the End Time was near. Six million Jews, *God's chosen people*, exterminated. He could barely get his head around that one. And in his own neighborhood, a murder every day. Stealing. Lying. Coveting another man's woman like it was some kind of game. The list of human cruelties would take you a million lifetimes to recite.

So St. James wrote ten new commandments for the world. But he wrote them in his own invented language, a series of loops and cursive-looking shapes that occasionally resembled letters. After his death, among stacks of paper, there were some legible notes found. Among them were these messages: "This is true that the great Moses the giver of the tenth commandment appeared in Washington, D.C., April 11, 1931." "This is true that on October 2, 1946, the great Virgin Mary and the Star of Bethlehem appeared over the nation's capital." "This is true that Adam the first man God created appeared in person on January 20, 1949. This was on the day of President Truman's inauguration." "This design [*The Throne*] is proof of the Virgin Mary descending [*sic*] into Heaven, November 2, 1950. It is also spoken of by Pope Pius XII."

He also wrote a new book of Revelation. Like St. John's Revelation in the New Testament, recorded in a special language on the Isle of Patmos and scribbled onto parchment at the speed of a fever dream, St. James's Revelation was also a kind of stenography from God. On fire with the Spirit when he wrote, he recorded these messages in a spiral notebook. On the cover, in blue U.S.-government ink, was scribbled *The Book of the 7 Dispensation* by St. James. Scholars have deemed the book, like the commandments, illegible. The few English words that appear in it, such as "Revelation" and "Virgin Mary," are most often in all caps and misspelled.

vi.

"And I saw a new heaven and a new earth: the first heaven and the first earth were passed away . . ." (*Revelation* 21:1)

He knew what that meant, knew the third heaven was the heaven of God, the second heaven was the heaven of the stars and the sun and the moon, and the first heaven, the doomed heaven spoken of in *Revelation*, was here, now. He was preparing.

He worked through the dark mornings, his joints and back tight as rusty hinges in the damp cold of the garage. Sometimes he'd stop to draw a quick sketch of a plan or to stare at what he was making.

He had built a stage in the back of the garage on which to set some of the pieces. On the larger objects he put rusty metal casters so he could move them to just the right spot. Everything was perfectly symmetrical, had to be, because St. James was remaking time. That's right, remaking time. Not just representing time as told in the Bible, he was replicating it with trash. You can see it if you look. On the right is the story of the Old Testament, of Moses and the Law; on the left is the history of Jesus and Grace, the way to salvation.

St. James understood that the time of God, the only time, was cyclical, always returning. No thing, no event, was pointless. Life repeated. It was right there in *Ecclesiastes*: "The sun also ariseth, and the sun goeth down, and hasteth to his place where he arose . . . The thing that hath been, it is that which shall be; and that which is done is that which shall be done." Death simply meant rebirth and a new, more glorious life in heaven, where you would be reunited with all things lost, with Lee and your father and some of the men from the 385th who had died since the war. If you placed your faith in the Lord Jesus Christ you would never, ever die. Your tears would be wiped away and forgotten. If you placed your faith in Jesus it didn't matter that you cleaned toilets and lived alone, that sometimes the people on your street scared you, called you a crazy fuck, a hermit, that sometimes the voices in your head called you things even worse, things you didn't want to hear; and it didn't matter that so many of the people you loved had vanished from the earth and your life and you could actually feel the empty spaces they left behind. None of it mattered. And if you truly believed, you were not just a poor man alone in the city among the poor, toiling in a poorly lit garage, babbling to a brick wall; you were not just a janitor, a forgotten vet scraping by on a paltry check. Your life mattered now and forever. Your life actually mattered.

He worked. He covered bottles and jelly jars and lightbulbs with gold and silver foil, which he got from wine bottles and imported beer bottles and cigarette cartons and boxes of aluminum wrap. He used the tops of coffee cans for bases. He mounted upside-down drawers on cheap glass vases, wrapped them in foil. He trimmed the edges of a sawed-in-half table with government electrical cable before covering it all in gold foil. He used kraft paper and cardboard for angels' wings, used carpet rolls to support the greatest weight. He used glue and nails and pins, and sometimes he encased an object in layers of foil until it was exactly the right size and shape.

And then there was *The Throne* itself, the centerpiece of the huge structure, an old red-plush chair bought secondhand. He gave it gold wings and put it up high, a seat for the coming Savior. He gave it a high back—four feet, five feet?—of wooden shapes and smaller cardboard wings and bulbs of silver and gold. He named objects for saints and tacked his walls with biblical quotes and a picture of Lee, who was now, God told him, an angel living inside His body, God's body as big as eternity. At the top of it all, this expanse that filled the entire back of a cold, damp garage at the end of a dark alley in one of the roughest neighborhoods in the city of Washington were the words "Fear Not."

vii.

St. James left the earth before he was ready, before he was finished, even though he once told the merchant he rented the garage from, "*The Throne* is my life. I'll finish it before I die." He had been working on it in the garage for fourteen years, thinking about it perhaps forever, and he wasn't done. He had had stomach cancer for some time, though it had only recently been diagnosed at the free clinic for World War vets. He refused to believe he was dying. It wasn't his time yet. He worked on *The Throne* up to the very end. The work eased his pain.

sentimental,

heartbroken rednecks

Unless a writer is extremely old when he dies, in which case he has probably become a neglected institution, his death must always seem untimely. This is because a real writer is always shifting and changing and searching. The world has many labels for him, of which the most treacherous is the label of Success.

—James Baldwin, "Alas, Poor Richard"

i.

I came across *The Stories of Breece D'J Pancake*, a bent-spined book wedged back among other fictions, while not shelving at a university library when I was twenty. My job, before they "asked me to leave," was late-shift shelver. I chose to work the late shift because no supervisors and very few students were around. My non-shelving went like this: At nine each night I would take a full cart of books—a big, scratched, wooden thing with whistling black wheels the size of golf balls—up to the fourth floor (Quiet Study), find a secluded aisle, and, picking books nearly at random from the shelves or from the cart I wasn't going to unload, read first sentences until I found just the right tone and rhythm—sometimes the hard declarative got me, other times a windy, baroque sentence—then sit down and read for a few hours. It was the most edifying minimum-wage job from which one could ever hope to get soundly and swiftly canned.

I picked up this particular book—let's say it was a Tuesday night, air filled with the soft electric drone of a library, a fat moon hovering in the blue window at the end of the aisle—because of the unique name down the spine: Breece D'J Pancake. I had to skip the foreword by Pulitzer Prize winner James Alan McPherson, of whom I had never heard, to get to the real first sentence, in a story called "Trilobites": "I open the truck's door, step onto the brick side street."

I liked the simplicity, the economy—the speed that comma generated in the middle of the sentence. I fancied myself someone who might one day put a pickup truck and a brick side street in an opening sentence, someone who would write stories full of brokenhearted loners, based entirely on the people I knew in Virginia, people who drank Bud and either worked hard or didn't work at all and never, no matter what, said what they felt because whatever that might be was surely killing them; these were people who in fact could not muster whatever it is inside a human being that allows one to reason through and articulate thoughts and feelings. I was going to devote my life to doing it for them.

The characters that crowded my skull back then fumbled through meaningless lives toward ambiguously meaningful acts of depravity and violence, acts entirely and only in *my* control, acts, I hoped, a reader would understand as profoundly significant even if the character went on wallowing in darkness. At twenty I had theories and thoughts in surplus, most of which ended in fantasies of me as famous and thoroughly praised for my deep insight.

In memory—which tends to be fluid and nostalgic, if not downright false—I knew Pancake was a Southerner eleven words in. I felt that largely irrational regional kinship Southerners (or rather writers, critics, and commentators from the South) expend so much energy talking about.

I read on, down through the first paragraph, struck by the honed sentences, the linguistic tension, the somber tone, the imagery: "The air is smoky with summertime. A bunch of starlings swim over me ... I remember Pop's dead eyes looking at me. They were real dry, and that took something out of me."

I read the twelve stories in the book during my shift (one of my last, it turned out). They were all about outsiders, the working poor of the craggy hills of West Virginia, just a couple of hours from where I live in the Blue Ridge Mountains, a land of satellite dishes on hilltops and the skeletons of rusty pickups slumped uselessly in ivy-filled ravines, a land of leaning trailers and primer-colored cars up on blocks.

Critic Lewis Simpson, in *The Dispossessed Garden* (another book I lucked upon; with enough leisure and curiosity, one can luck one's way right through an entire library wing), wrote: "Southern fiction derive[s] from visions in which faith in the [writer's] ability to make his own world has had an entangled confrontation with an experience of memory and history that tells him he cannot do it." In other words, the writer begins with failure and pushes forward from there—the central metaphor of Original Sin further complicated by family, community, and shared history. This was certainly true of Pancake's stories. They were exhausting exercises in hope and futility, struggle and failure, and, ultimately, in figuring out how to carry on for the next struggle, which was always, though played out in physical terms, moral in nature.

Some of the stories puzzled me. They were open-ended, both bleak and oddly reassuring about the central decency in humans, each offering a kind of raw immediacy and a stunted epiphany. His characters were bighearted dreamers, people trying to do right, yet stymied by economic woes, familial attachment, even the unforgiving landscape of Appalachia. They couldn't win; life presented them with failure and dead dreams as soon as they slithered into the world: from here, they began. I knew what he meant. I felt a little dead back then, reading those stories, cloaked in failure.

It's the old story of Southern art, the one I've been aware of all my life, I guess, the one you can read in Faulkner, O'Connor, and Welty, the one you can hear in the songs of Hank Williams, Johnny Cash, Lucinda Williams, and Steve Earle: *We're utterly defeated, doomed to live out our genealogical and historical unhappiness, but not without a bloody sort of passion and genuine tears.* We celebrate the noble fuckup, the hero as lost cause. And like the above-named artists, Pancake's greatest strength as a writer was to render in words a moment, toward the end of each story—stories oddly akin to good country songs, to sad ballads—of uncomfortably authentic pain and confession, a moment when reader and writer unite within character, creating—ever so briefly—a perfect, universal instant of empathy.

The stories were tragic to the extreme, biblical in power, yet they possessed a rare honesty and vulnerability. The style was Sherwood Anderson or Ernest Hemingway—spare, yet poetic, hard, and direct.

I took the book home that night to read the foreword and afterword, to find out about Breece Pancake.

ii.

By the time I was reading the foreword and afterword that evening when I was twenty, Pancake had been dead for twelve years. Four years before the posthumous publication of *The Stories of Breece D'J Pancake*, on Palm Sunday, 1979, he sat in a lawn chair behind his apartment in Charlottesville, Virginia, where he had attended graduate school, and placed the butt of an over-and-under .20-gauge shotgun on the soft wet ground in front him. He leaned forward, letting the steel barrel click against his teeth, and pulled the trigger. He was twenty-six.

Four years later, had he been alive, he would have realized the major success he had always dreamed of, the fame and thorough praise for his insight, standing at the forefront of a virtual renaissance in Appalachian fiction that included such writers as Bobbie Ann Mason, Jayne Anne Phillips, Cormac McCarthy, and Denise Giardina.

I've thought of Pancake a lot since then. I've read his best stories—"Trilobites," "Hollow," "In the Dry," "The Honored Dead"—over and over with admiration, always stunned by their precision and sincerity. The people he wrote about, his people, as the idiom goes, are much like my people. I see some of what I think of as my place in his place. And, sometimes frighteningly, I see myself, the writer, in a shared context with him, the writer.

I understand that the better one gets at writing, the more one can do with language, form it and reform it like so much clay, pack it with density or strip it down, the harder writing gets, the more your own sentences can sound like bullshit and lies in your head, the more your failures—which frankly almost no one but you even cares about— can weigh you down psychically and depress you.

I graduated from the creative writing program at the University of Virginia two decades after Pancake did, held the same fellowship, walked through the same halls, studied with some of the same professors. And though there is always a macabre pull to focus on the tragic, grisly, and sad—I feel it right now—it is Pancake's small body of work and his life that have always interested me: how his life not only informed his writing, but was his writing.

iii.

He thought of himself as a work in progress, and he was hard on his work, hard on himself as a worker. His mother, Helen Pancake, in a letter to James Alan McPherson concerning the publication of *The Stories* in 1983 by Little, Brown, wrote, "Jim, 'bullshit' was one of B's choice sayings—in fact he used to say he wanted his short stories entitled 'Bullshit Artist.' Love his heart!"

Here was a young writer who would often write fifteen to twenty drafts of a story (long before word processors, when you had to literally rewrite a story), struggled every day with the craft of writing, every second, it seems, pondering the large moral questions he addressed in his work. Considering the importance he placed on his fiction, a remark like "bullshit artist," even if said with an aw-shucks grin, shows just how self-deprecating he could be. When your work is your life, losing faith in it means you can't look in the mirror.

Many people, including National Book Award–winning novelist John Casey, who still teaches one

semester a year at the University of Virginia, have
called Pancake an "aristocrat in blue jeans," a
young man "wise beyond his years," concerned
with an older set of values and traditions from Appalachia, those handed over from Europe and early
Christianity and then cordoned off by geographic
isolation and small and all but static populations.
Statements like these, coupled with his still-
fragmented biography, have surrounded the life
and work of Pancake with an almost James Dean–
like mythology among writers and Southern and
Appalachian literary scholars.

By all accounts, though, he did view himself as
chivalrous, striving for a kind of Old World nobility in a time when notions of nobility had more
to do with material acquisition and upbringing
than character or deeds. He thought of life as
something to face with your fists clenched and
then conquer, and he would come to think of his
fictions as a kind of mission—the most important
thing he had—to mine the depths of himself and
the world to get at what was real and pure and
vital. To dispense, in fact, with bullshit.

iv.

Pancake was born in Milton, West Virginia, in
1952 as Breece Dexter Pancake. He attended West

Virginia Wesleyan in Buckhannon for two years, then graduated from Marshall University in 1974. He spent time traveling out West, working odd jobs, then took a position teaching English at Fork Union Military Academy (where, twenty-three years later, I would be offered—and would decline—the same job), forty miles southeast of Charlottesville. In January of 1975, he began attending John Casey's writing workshop at the University of Virginia. Casey saw him as prodigiously talented, and he and Pancake would later become close friends.

Many things happened in 1975 that greatly changed Pancake's life. His father, C. R. Pancake, died of complications from multiple sclerosis on September 8 in Milton. Less than three weeks later, on September 29, Pancake's longtime best friend and drinking buddy, Matthew Heard, was killed in a gruesome high-speed car accident in West Virginia. In October, still reeling and angry and sad and vulnerable, he met award-winning Southern novelists Mary Lee Settle and Peter Taylor, relationships he would keep and foster until his death four years later.

In one year, Pancake must have felt that he had lost everything and at the same time gained a new life. Most of the baggage and connections to home were gone, vanished in an instant. And suddenly some of the best writers in the country at ostensibly one of the best writing programs in the country viewed him as the real thing, an artist, seemed, in fact, to admire his work in a way they might a peer's as opposed to a student's.

Months later he was officially accepted to both the Iowa Writers' Workshop and the writing program at the University of Virginia, choosing the latter. He was on his way, wishing his father and Matthew were around to see it.

v.

In the foreword to *The Stories*, McPherson describes Pancake as "constitutionally . . . a lonely and melancholy man." Certainly now, after the loss of his father and best friend, he was even more so.

In Charlottesville, where he finally moved in 1976, he lived in a dingy one-room apartment at 1 Blue Ridge Lane (where there is now a neighborhood of half-million-dollar homes and a nearby country club). His desk, where he kept the many drafts of his stories, was a piece of plywood set up on sawhorses in a corner.

He kept to himself, as always, gregarious on a superficial level but never letting anyone get too close to him. If he thought he was making someone uncomfortable with his loud voice or Southern drawl, he would apologize politely and vanish, go off by himself and not be heard from for days.

In Charlottesville, which is in one of the wealthiest counties in the United States, and at the University of Virginia, which is notoriously conservative (in the relative world of universities) and filled, it seems, with the upwardly mobile children of America's most privileged, Pancake stuck out like, well, a six-foot-plus, bearded West Virginian with an accent that connoted the lower classes, wearing old blue jeans, a leather jacket, and a pair of shit-kicker cowboy boots; this among a student population with an inordinate number of young people who have attended operas, polo matches, and debutante balls throughout their lives.

I remember days of chilly vibes myself in those hallowed halls, and this was two decades later and, presumably, in a university with a now far more tolerant and diversified environment. I once attended a lecture by a stuffy and moderately famous poet in which he talked about the ingenious use of space in the trailers of the rural poor (for instance, you could put your child's Big Wheel on the kitchen counter when it was raining; this had somehow been turned into a post-structuralist book of some sort containing photographs and an abstruse, utterly condescending essay), and it was all I could do not to hurl a stack of books at him.

Pancake, to say the least, did not fit in at Mr. Jefferson's university. When he wasn't writing, or hunting or fishing or hiking in the Blue Ridge Mountains along the same Appalachian trails that begin just a few miles from my home, he spent most of his social time among other writers— McPherson and Casey particularly, who were also his teachers.

All writers, at least all the ones I know, regardless of background, gender, or ethnicity, tend to be outsiders to some degree, socially guarded, a little scorched on the inside, entranced by the world yet not quite trusting it completely, so he felt most comfortable among them and appreciated what they had to offer him—their experience, the names of authors that inspired them, a good stiff drink (interestingly, one of Pancake's favorite writers was Jack London, author of the blackly hilarious *Martin Eden*, which is about a writer who becomes successful and finds he much preferred his far more understandable and less maddening failure).

Also in 1976, he began going to the maximum-security prison in Jarratt to talk to and teach prisoners, eventually helping a young inmate publish some of his poetry. He considered this a duty, not charity, an Old World act of *noblesse oblige*.

For the most part, however, Pancake stayed true to his "lonely and melancholy" nature, leaning over his plywood desk at 1 Blue Ridge Lane, arranging and rearranging words and sentences until he felt they contained little pieces of his heart. Then he would put a line through them and begin again. They were all wrong.

vi.

In June of 1977, Pancake, who had been raised in what I'd call mild Protestantism—as opposed, say, to Southern Baptism or Seventh Day Adventism or other evangelical denominations common to his region of birth—converted to Catholicism, and he officially became a novitiate in the Church just before his twenty-fifth birthday.

He found in Catholicism the kind of rigid moral code he sought, one that did not bend to fit the shape of the cultural moment. He valued ideas and things from an older time, a time he'd only read about, and had little patience for ideological fads and trends. Though he was not, according to those closest to him, judgmental toward the behavior of others, it seems safe to say he became a staunch conservative.

The strictness of the Catholic Church—the

clearly defined values—coincided with what he expected from himself, what he explored in his stories. He took the Catholic name John (writer of the Book of Revelation), making himself Breece Dexter John Pancake.

A month earlier, in May, *The Atlantic* had accepted "Trilobites" for publication in their December issue. It was his first acceptance in a major magazine. But he didn't gloat, didn't become smug with success; rather, he doubted his ability to live up to his own high standards even more. He felt, in low moments, that he was a fraud, a true Martin Eden, and now he'd convinced an editor at a big, important magazine that he was somehow a real writer. Here is what he'd wanted—what he'd struggled for at that plywood desk with the pictures of his father and Matthew on it—and now he was sad and ridiculous because he suddenly knew that the people out there deeming literary work worthy or unworthy were utterly lacking in taste, possibly as fraudulent as he was. I think of Walker Percy's famous opening passage in *The Second Coming*: "In fact, he didn't even realize he was depressed. Rather was it the world and life around him which seemed to grow more senseless and farcical with each passing day."

When he received the check for the story, he

wired his mother flowers and took James Mc-
Pherson to dinner, where he drank like a man
drowning his sorrows. McPherson described him
on this night as far from pleased with himself, instead "morose and nervous." He felt like he'd just
been given the keys to the world, only to find out
that the world wasn't much.

He began working even harder—at writing, at
life; maybe that was the answer. Daniel Menaker
at *The New Yorker* solicited a story in November
of 1977. Pancake worked through mornings, drank
alone through most nights, never missed mass on
Sundays, prayed and doubted himself. In February,
The Atlantic accepted "In the Dry." In March,
Nightwork accepted "Time and Again." At twenty-
five he was quickly becoming the center of a literary buzz.

Around this time, he asked John Casey to be his
godfather in the Church. In the afterword of *The
Stories*, Casey writes: "This godfather arrangement
soon turned upside down. Breece started getting
after me about going to mass, going to confession,
instructing my daughters. It wasn't so much out of
righteousness as out of gratitude and affection, but
he could be blistering . . . As with his other knowledge and art, he took in his faith with intensity,
almost as if he had a different, deeper measure of
time. He was soon an older Catholic than I was."

In March of 1978, Wendy Jacobson, on the basis
of a couple of Pancake's stories, solicited a novel
for Doubleday. He began making notes, writing
character sketches, telling friends about his good
fortune, acting, in fact, like someone who expected to live a long time.

vii.

In 1983, *The Stories* were nominated for the Pulitzer Prize for fiction and the Weatherford Prize
for the best book about Appalachia. Joyce Carol
Oates, in *The New York Times*, compared the debut
to Hemingway's *In Our Time*. The critical acclaim
was overwhelming and unanimous. *The Stories of
Breece D'J Pancake* has never gone out of print. If
I try, I mean if I really try, I can almost consider
that a happy ending.

Henry Miller once said that literature was the
common life, examined and exalted. E. M. Cioran
intimated that only literature about the pauper or
the bum, the life all but lost, is interesting, because
the powerful in society are not even real but rather
figments or projections, elaborate constructs, with
important-sounding titles (I think what Cioran,
that poet of nihilism, meant is that deep down we
are all paupers, some of us just insist on perpetu-
ating the elaborate charade that we are not).

Sometimes I think they're talking about Pancake. He struggled on the page and in life. He examined and exalted in story after story, holding created lives still for a few tightly focused pages, distilling moments of chaos into instants of crystalline meaning and morose poetry.

But life is murkier—you can't contain it in the biggest book, can you?—hard on those who can't find temperance. Life is without rhetorical shape, regardless of how rigid your chosen system of values.

viii.

Pancake was a moralist, a sad humanist, in the strictest Christian sense. His characters begin, wearing Original Sin like their own flesh, caught up in a world where they seem destined to struggle and fail and pay for their failure—gospel music or blue grass chiseled into diamond-hard prose.

Pancake's favorite biblical verses were Revelation 3:15–16: "I know thy works, that thou art neither cold nor hot: I would thou wert cold or hot. So then because thou art lukewarm, and neither cold nor hot, I will spue thee out of my mouth."

Fitting verses for a writer, a man, who seems to have been nothing but cold or hot, yet always, dangerously, perceiving himself as lukewarm, somehow failing, failing, failing, savoring the acceptances and adulation for only a second and dwelling endlessly on—replaying in his head— every rejection and humiliating disappointment that any life of art, even the most successful one, is necessarily full of.

Pancake was hard on his characters, yes—a bit like pulling the wings off an insect and watching it bang its head against the inside of a jar—but he also always let them see, if only for a second, a glimpse of light in all that darkness. In the last line of perhaps his best-known story, "Trilobites," he sets a boy named Colley free of all that came before with a deceptively simple declarative statement: "I feel my fear moving away in rings through time for a million years."

He was not, however, so kind to himself.

In early 1979, he began giving all his possessions away; "gifts," he said, because he would be leaving Charlottesville soon. He had applied for a couple of writing fellowships with residencies, had some teaching opportunities, was working hard on the novel. Because he never let anyone get too close— not even Casey or McPherson—and given his extraordinary success at such a young age, friends thought he was fine; just Breece being Breece—

difficult as hell, always up for a good argument, hard-drinking and a little sad, but genuinely kind, decent, and generous.

He wrote an encouraging letter to a friend and fellow writer. On the envelope, Pancake had changed the return address from "1 Blue Ridge Lane" to "One Blow Out Your Brain." To another friend he wrote, "If I weren't a good Catholic, I'd consider getting a divorce from life." Yet it was only in hindsight that these messages were perceived as portentous (Pancake was famous for his black humor).

On Palm Sunday 1979, he used the only shotgun he hadn't given away to kill himself. I have no idea, nor does anyone, how intentional or accidental his suicide was, how deep-seated or fleeting his darkest thoughts. Maybe he'd been planning it since his father and Matthew died, or since that first story was accepted and he saw the beginnings of the absurd shape of success. Maybe, as Cheever once wrote, Pancake was "deeply conscious of chaos, as if we were in the act of falling from some atmospheric and moral orbit, as if the sweet seriousness of life were in great danger." Maybe he only thought he meant it and his finger moving, that slight expulsion of digital energy while he held the cold, oil-smelling steel in his mouth, was a mistake.

Whatever happened, whatever you want to believe, he pulled the trigger. He died.

He was found by a neighbor with the shotgun still in his hands, his body slumped in a lawn chair under an apple tree, his head flung back, face aimed heavenward.

I could show you right where it happened.

a stupid story

*K*ids lined up *along the sidewalks. Shuffling in the cold. Under these factories. Smells like raw sewage. God, it's like they're knee-deep in their own crap. Smell that? No place to hang out, if you ask me. But what the hell do I know, right, old guy like me?*

Want one? Don't smoke? Fine. Suit yourself.

My boy Jimbo used to hang out here. His name was Jim, actually James, but I called him Jimbo since he was young. Used to be one of them, standing right down there all the time.

No, just a little farther up.

One time I picked up a kid right here. Right about here. I merged over toward the kids, cutting across the left lane, to pull up along the curb like a regular, like

125

someone out for a blow. Some bitch honked at me and shot the finger. If I was someone else, or maybe if it'd just been a few months earlier, I don't know, I might have blown her away. Seriously, I might have shot her. Bitch, know what I mean? Sure you do. You don't just go beeping and shooting the bird at people. What world do you live in, lady? People get shot. You wouldn't do that. Right? It's stupid. Exactly. Crazy. Down here, too. Yeah. (Laughter.) Dead in the sewage. (Laughter.) Dumb bitch.

Anyway, traffic was real bad that evening. Taillights here to there. Could smell gas in the car with you. Even though it was winter, windows rolled up, heat on. True story: kid in my neighborhood goes to the hospital after falling asleep with a gas-soaked rag over his face, trying to get high. Same kid is now almost thirty, walks around town with a Walkman on, smiling. Walks like twenty miles a day. Still lives at home, in a room above the garage. Never had a job. True story. Swear to God. You ought to write that down.

That day I pulled up to the curb, and I caught a wheel on the sidewalk and then dropped off, making all the kids look. Some laughed. I felt a little stupid. I was kinda nervous. I'll give you that.

I rolled down my window.

Yeah, said a kid with those weird dreadlocks. Right, like that, like, I don't know, cigars or something. 'Bout yea long.

Anyway, Hi, I said. I pointed to the kid I'd seen before, a few days earlier. He was sitting against the fence, looking sort of lost, like Jimbo. He seemed perfect, like a stunt double, swear to God. He looked like someone who'd hang himself in a second. I said to the kid in my window, Him. I pointed. Over there, I said. Could you get him for me?

Kid turned and yelled, Beano! This guy wants you.

He said "wants" like I was the world's biggest perv, spanking it in my car already.

Beano looked around, hesitated a sec, then stood up and walked over to my window. His breath was like exhaust hissing out of his nose it was so cold. He had on a hooded sweatshirt and a hat on backward, Padres, or maybe Orioles. Black. I couldn't believe the resemblance. I couldn't believe it.

He goes, What?

I smiled. I couldn't believe it. I know, I said that. But I couldn't believe it. Just like Jimbo, my boy, with all this attitude.

I was wondering if you wanted to make a few bucks, I said.

Nah, man, I ain't like that, he said. Those kids are down there—he pointed behind me—on the next corner.

It'll take about an hour. I'll give you fifty bucks. I showed him a crisp fifty, like this. Nothing sexual, I said. That ain't me. And it ain't right.

What then? he goes.

Get in and we'll talk. You won't have to do anything.

Right, man. You'll try to eat my eyeballs or something, Mr. Dahmer. That's what he called me, Mr. Dahmer.

Fifty bucks. And I ain't going to touch you. I was real stern, real serious about that. I ain't a perv. You know that. You can see that. I'm fifty. I gotta good job. I gotta wife. I pay taxes, a registered Republican. I don't go for boys. You write that down, you put that in there.

I don't know, he goes. He looked around.

Fifty. I held up the bill again, like this.

You touch me, you make a move, and you'll be sorry. My dad's a cop.

I go, Hey, I won't lay a hand on you.

Seriously, he goes, pointing at me, getting in. If I say the word, you let me out.

We drove to St. Anne's. I was thinking about Jimbo. I was sweating a little under my arms. Just a little bit, even though it was cold. He kinda gave me the creeps. Sitting there. I'm not going to lie. I was thinking about my boy, my son, and getting pretty sad but I didn't want this new kid, Beano, to know I was sad so I put on the radio station Jimbo used to like, I mean back when he would talk to me, and pushed in the lighter and lit a smoke and offered Beano one, too. Want one? No still, huh? Suit yourself. You like that station? I like country. Old stuff. This? I don't know what the hell this is. But, hey, you like it, I'll keep it on.

Anyway, Beano took the smoke and asked me what I wanted from him.

I want you to be my son, I said, and later, you know, when I started really thinking about all this, when I started thinking that maybe it'd be nice to talk to someone about this, I kept going back to the way I said that. I mean, I'm not trying to get all psychoanalytical or anything but that's just a weird way to put it, you know. I'm like the next guy. I ain't immune to stuff. I feel things.

What? Beano goes.

Act like my son, I go.

You mean pretend to be your son? Beano goes.

Yeah. Is it that complicated? Fifty bucks. Half an hour. No big deal.

For what?

What?

What do you want me to pretend I'm your son for?

His grandma. My wife's mother. She loved my son Jimbo. She always asks about him. My wife already told her, but she's, you know, out of it. She's old and half crazy. She won't remember. She can't remember one minute to the next.

See, I guess I thought I was going to be a hero. I felt like I needed to do something nice—for me, for Nana, for Jimbo, even for my wife maybe. I don't know. Why am I talking about this shit? You ever feel like that, like you need to do something decent? I grew up real religious.

Baptist. Don't mess with a Baptist, man. Christ. Fire and brimstone. Satan just like embedded in the particles in the air or something. You should put down that I'm religious. Because I am. I love God plenty. I ask him stuff sometimes. Like, Hey, God, how did everything get so fucked up?

Wait a minute, Beano goes. Jimbo's dead?

Nah nah, I said. I paused. I got kinda, I don't know, you know, like, some kind of, I don't know. Nothing like that, I said, he's just . . . unavailable.

But if your wife already told the old lady, maybe it ain't such a good idea.

You want the money or no? I say.

We were almost there at that point, a few blocks from here; know where it is? Right.

Beano looked out the window. Headlights were bright in the sideview mirror, which was right below his chin from this angle. I was looking like this. He was sitting right there, where you are.

Real quiet he goes, Yeah, I want the money. Just saying.

I lit another cigarette, asked if he wanted one.

No. Don't worry. I ain't going to ask you again.

Then he goes, right out of the blue, You divorced?

None of your business, I said. Then: No, I ain't divorced. I said I was married, didn't I?

All right, man. Not like I care. Just seems like you're probably divorced. Seems like you live alone, is all.

I'm married, I said, like I told you. For now. Then I figured I didn't owe this kid an explanation. I said, Things are just a little weird. Me and my wife have a lot on our minds.

He looked over at me. Yeah. Just pay me my fifty like you promised.

St. Anne's. You can never find a parking space. I drive laps. Laps. It gives me a headache every time I come, if you want to know.

Nana, my wife's mother, who was really like my one and only mother during the whole early part of our marriage before she had a stroke and then all the complications and then just got all old and senile and incoherent, was up on the fifth floor, in a private room that was costing my wife and I our whole retirement. When it rains it pours, know what I mean? That could be your title. When It Rains It Pours. Or: John Barclay: Everything He Touches Turns to Shit.

Me and Beano got on the elevator and went up and didn't say anything the whole way. He fidgeted just like Jimbo. I wondered if he took anything, any medications; I wondered what he thought about, if he thought, you know, bad stuff, sad stuff, whatever, I don't know. But I didn't ask because I wanted this to be as simple as possible.

Now I'm not even going to get into the stuff about Nana, tell you about the machines and her expressions and the bed pans and the sour smell of dying people, and so on. It's depressing. Depressing. Horrible is what it is. Life. Christ. I don't know. Jesus. Push in the lighter there. Satan in air particles. What about that? (Laughs, uncomfortably.)

I can't save people from what goes on in their heads and make their lives all peachy. I mean, what am I? I'm a kid's dad and I'm supposed to be able to fix his whole life. He wouldn't even talk to me. I'm supposed to make my wife want to dance. What? What am I? What am I? Who the fuck am I? I'm this fat old guy. I got a job. I got stuff to do. I wish I could change things. I'd fix everything, I'd fix everybody, I swear to God, I would, I'd do it. I'd save my marriage, make time move backward. If I could, I'd erase whole years and then do it all over again, but prepared this time, tuned in to the little stuff I missed the first time. My life ain't peachy. You don't see me hanging myself in a shed. That's just selfish, if you ask me, that's just trying to hurt the people who love you and make them feel guilty is all.

All right. Sorry. I'm rambling. Keep that up and I might start to look really bad, huh?

So Beano sat in Nana's room and I told Nana that Beano was my son Jimbo. Jimbo was doing really great in school. He was probably going to go to college. He was on the debate team, football, all kinds of bullshit.

I whispered to Beano to tell Nana that he loved her. Why not? Jimbo maybe would have. I doubt it. But maybe. Fifty, I whispered.

I love you, Nana, Beano said, but he was looking at me and he was turning a little pink. He didn't sound convincing.

I pointed at her and gave him a face like, Come on.

He leaned over her then, like he really meant it, and said, real sincere, too, Nana, I love you. I wondered who he said that to for real. If anyone. I got that kind of mind, you know. I wonder what people are thinking, what they might say if given the opportunity. Some people say I'm philosophical.

She said, Oh I love you, too, Jim. You're my best boy. Nana loves her Jim.

Her face is all wrinkled but God it was, well, it was something. Nearly killed me, kid. That one nearly took my head right off.

Then a few other things happened—a nurse came in, I turned on the TV and me and Beano and Nana watched Wheel of Fortune. *One of the puzzles was* COOKIES IN THE COOKIE JAR; *another was* GOOD-BYE BLUE SKY. *I got both right away, before the Amway rep from Syracuse or the teacher or whatever from Phoenix or Philadelphia or Fargo. Then we left. That was basically it.*

So I brought Beano back down here. I gave him the fifty and he got out. We didn't say anything. A deal's a deal in my book. I promise, I deliver.

Then Beano stopped on the sidewalk and turned and looked at me like he wanted to say something.

I rolled down the window.

He looked at his shoes, scuffed something on the concrete. He was a nervous kid.

He goes, I'm sorry about your son, man.

I didn't say anything. He looked at me. I nodded. He walked off. I drove home.

I don't know. It's a stupid story, isn't it? I don't think this means anything. But if you polish it up, maybe.

This is really just something I tell people sometimes. Not like I dwell on it. This is just a story I tell people. You know, to talk.

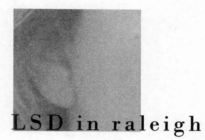

LSD in raleigh

Under these circumstances there was no question of
loneliness.

—Walter Benjamin, "Hashish in Marseilles"

I *once spent two days on LSD.* This
was in Raleigh, North Carolina, in 1991. I
was twenty. It was during the first Lollapalooza
festival put on by Perry Farrell and headlined by
his band, Jane's Addiction, the finest art-rock band,
I used to say back then, since Ziggy Stardust and
the Spiders from Mars or the New York Dolls.

I took three hits of acid, total. A girl with
mustard-smelling fingers whose name I cannot remember softly placed the first small, square piece
of paper on my tongue. We were standing in a
cheap motel room that smelled faintly of old
smoke and foreign bodies, of sex and something
sweetly medicinal. I took the second hit that night
while pacing alone around a parking lot between

a Denny's and a Howard Johnson's, overly intrigued by how the humidity turned the high
streetlights into glowing orbs the exact size of the
moon, how the rain glazed cars in a Vaseline
sheen, and the bright neon orange of the Howard
Johnson's sign was the gaping mouth of a volcano.
I took the third hit the morning of the festival,
while standing in front of a steel, water-spotted
bathroom mirror in a Wilco gas station, staring at
the intricate hair patterns in my eyebrows.

That day the world glowed, an endless halo that
quivered with new meanings. My body was filled
with hot helium. Gravity showed me a kindness
and mercy I didn't know it had. Pretense was
flayed away from each thing and person. Self-
consciousness was a hundred pounds of chain mail
I hadn't known I was wearing.

But I can't write about it, about the day,
about tripping. I mean, really write about it. I can't
capture the essence of the thing itself, the experience. I'm left with representation, symbols, metaphors, similes, words that hold some poetic or
intellectual cultural associations that I can attempt
to arrange in such a way that might evoke some
semblance of how I felt. But it's bullshit; it's ap-
proximation.

There is a reason why writing about drugs, from Baudelaire to Burroughs and beyond, almost always trundles off into the familiarly banal, the cliché. There is a gap—a chasm—between raw experience and representation, most especially in regard to narcosis, but, frankly, in regard to everything. Our resources—language and the philosophy implicit within it—are limited. It's like trying to talk about God, or love, or psychic pain without sounding like a fool.

The English philosopher C. D. Broad (professor of moral philosophy, Trinity College, Cambridge, from 1933 to 1953, interested in the "scientific evidence for survival after death") once wrote, ". . . the function of the brain and nervous system . . . is in the main *eliminative* and not productive. Each person is at each moment capable of remembering all that has ever happened to him and of perceiving everything that is happening everywhere in the universe. The function of the brain and nervous system is to protect us from being overwhelmed and confused by this mass of largely useless and irrelevant knowledge, by shutting out most of what we should otherwise perceive or remember at any moment, and leaving only that very small and special selection which is likely to be practically useful."

The insane, the tripping, and, I suppose, the visionary lose this "protective" or "eliminative" function. You step outside the world of symbols, out beyond the boundaries of what can be represented, and this, I believe, is why so much writing about the hallucinogenic experience quakes with the emptily reverential/faux spiritual and bad poetry: the task, this task, is impossible.

The world that day, having changed none in makeup but enormously in meaning, suddenly seemed infinitely bigger. Schopenhauer's famous *The World as Will and Idea* implicitly touches on this sentiment: the world is not the world but simply our experience of the world. William Blake wrote the famous line (giving name to both a band and a book): "If the doors of perception were cleansed every thing would appear to man as it is, infinite." Aldous Huxley, starting with Blake's sentiment, wrote: "That which, in the language of religion, is called 'this world' is the universe of reduced awareness, expressed, and, as it were, petrified by language." Huxley (because he was a writer) goes on to point out that both art and religion would be obsolete if we could live according to Blake's sentiment: "Art, I suppose, is only for beginners, or else for those resolute dead-enders, who have made up their minds to be content with the *ersatz* of Suchness, with symbols rather than with what they signify, with the elegantly composed recipe in lieu of actual dinner." What I realized on three hits of acid, as the world flooded in and out of me, nearly stealing my breath, was how pitifully small my thoughts and feelings had always been.

I was starting to see—meaning, *think about in some slightly complex way*—the "horrors of drugs," how they ruined people's lives, how my own life hovered in a kind limbo because of them, how the insular yet expansive universe of drugs in suburban America where I lived was one of constant lies and cruelly absurd occurrences, how kids I knew got locked up for a bag of coke or 'shrooms or speed or crank or pot, or hung themselves in a shed, or got their girlfriends pregnant and denied it, or called up their old girlfriend and fired a shotgun into the ceiling of their tattered apartment (paid for by their parents) so she'd think it was a suicide, or decided to stand on the hood of a Jeep going sixty on a dark, desolate road, and so on and so on.

There are so many examples, so many things I was thinking about, obsessed with, back then, when I put all that acid on my tongue. There was the kid who overdosed on heroin in his friend's game room (later found by the friend's father, an air force officer); or the one who held up an Applebee's in Greenville, North Carolina, with a toy gun, which he decided to do, the story went, to pay off pot debts (this was later featured on a short-lived reality-TV program which featured an ending shot of the young man shouting "This one's for you, Dad" into the camera. I thought, *Wow, I used to get high with him*). Or there was the guy, who used to hang out with my brother, who stole his mother's VCR and hocked it for a rock of crack; or the kid named Jason, whom I once stole a bunch of stuff from a neighbor's house with for no better reason than simply to see if we could do it, who gave his car to a huge black guy for drugs (I can only imagine the lie he told his father, standing at a pay phone in a black ghetto, with no car, shaking as the high wore off).

I had spent the six weeks before Lollapalooza driving around the country with money I'd made working construction, a low-grade sadness coursing through me like a virus, sleeping in national forests in Idaho, Colorado, Montana, and Utah, bathing in rivers, doing the young bohemian thing as I vaguely understood and imagined it, reading what I figured were the underground classics—drug narratives, mostly—I needed to have committed to memory.

Now here I was in Raleigh, tripping, with a head full of books and more than a little anxiety

and melancholy over the state of basically everything—my life and the lives spinning out of control all around me. Looking back, I realize I was
primed for a very bad trip.

There were thousands and thousands of
people there, the music was blasting—Siouxsie &
the Banshees, Nine Inch Nails, Living Colour,
N.W.A., Jesus & Mary Chain, the Butthole Surf-
ers, Jane's Addiction—but I was off by myself,
wandering around the Hardee's Amphitheater,
into it, into all the beautiful minutiae that were
newly important to me, yet I was strangely outside
of the event itself, outside of social norms, even
outside of the governing structures of time. I was
lost inside my own skull.

The amphitheater was like a big shallow-grade
pit with seats in it, the stage down at the bottom;
around the pit/seats, in the back, was a long, green
grassy hill. Because in my state I couldn't hang out
with any of my drug friends—sadly lingering
friendships from high school based upon all sorts
of erroneous things—or focus on anything but my
own thoughts and the interesting stimuli around
me—an orange tent rope, a nipple ring, a squashed
grasshopper near a paper cup with chewing-
tobacco spit in it, the rise and fall of some black-

painted toenails coming toward me—I went to the top of the hill and started flipping down it.

I won't try to unravel the complex series of impulses and feelings ("thoughts" would be the wrong word) that brought me to this action because it would be impossible. But people cheered me on, probably with a little maliciousness, a little schadenfreude, in their hearts, hoping they might see me go away in one of the ambulances parked near the exits.

Go, motherfucker.

Yeah, man.

Get it, freak.

And of course I knew that these people thought I was insane, thought, probably, that I was, as I was, out of my mind, but I didn't care, because suddenly the gaze of others, as they say in graduate school, really didn't bother me at all. I felt sorry for them because they didn't understand how important this was, how there was a perfect sync to my movements, how I understood things about the grass and myself and movement and energy that they, sadly, would never, ever understand. I began humming an electrical tune I felt mostly in my lips and throat.

I've always worried, been a little petrified, about what people might think, if they think I'm smart or cool or funny, but not today, not at all; I was rolling rolling rolling, flipping flipping flipping, and then getting up at the bottom of the hill, which was seventy-five steep yards, and throwing my hands up and laughing—the spectacle, the freak, the schizophrenic off his meds—overcome with the joy of flipping, as unself-conscious as I was when I was a little boy and my mother used to sit in a lawn chair in front of our little brick house and watch me roll through the grass singing because I was flooded with life, totally consumed by the moment but at the same time not at all aware that I was consumed by the moment (a prerequisite of being consumed by the moment). This part of the day was like that part of childhood, early on, when you're getting the first glimmers of what will become adult consciousness and reasoning, when everything, the wide universe, has the ability to astonish, to delight or horrify, and each moment offers the possibility of something entirely new.

After flipping, I started doing long laps around the amphitheater, walking quickly with just shorts and sandals and sunglasses on, not panicked but needing to move. The sun blazed down on me. The crowds were made of color.

Everything, all prior meaning, even at the most basic level, was gone. No, not gone, exactly—*subsumed* into something much larger and scarier but also far more delicate and beautiful. The world was vast and different. The insignificant—a white spot on the fingernail of a vendor—was vital, worth what felt like hours of my mind's energy (though it may have been only seconds). That which was vital in the straight world—my being cool, striking some practiced pose I was barely conscious of—was now so trivial, so small and confining, that it didn't even register. Who cared about music and grooving with your friends when there were these . . . *brick patterns that signified the perfection of nature, the existence of a loving God* . . . Or when the huge screen behind the stage was actually made of . . . *little blinking colored squares that were exactly attuned to every feeling in the range of human emotions present here today,* moving and changing at an amazing speed, proving, once and for all, that there was such a thing as humanity—I mean, you know, like we were one big *organism,* each one of us just tiny cells intricately, inextricably connected.

The floodgates, the eliminative or protective mental narrowing functions, were gone in a dangerous way. I was out beyond the limits of language, where thoughts and feelings were no longer separate things evoking each other but in fact the same thing coming in at higher, stronger frequencies.

I was only in this most intense state for a couple

of hours. Then I started, slowly, to come down, to ease my way back into the familiar workings of the world. I was still extremely affected by the drug, but I at least remembered who and where I was, had some battered sense of ego creeping around, like a big wet worm, inside me.

There was a lot of political stuff going on, I remember, tents and booths, so now I went and got pamphlets about women's rights and tortured people in Third World countries and how technological progress was being perpetrated on the backs of Mother Earth and the poor, but the whole time I was thinking that there was no issue but love, which sounds ridiculous now as I say it— cliché drug-speak of the first order—but when I thought it then it was as tight and logical and true as a complex math problem finally solved. The grand answers to everything were this basic. Environmental problems—love! Torture—love! Oppression, repression, cruelty, emptiness, lies—love! I asked a meaty fraternity guy, the one person I might choose to hate for no good reason in that crowd, if he would hug me. And he did while all his friends laughed and shouted, *Faggots!*

Later I looked around and saw people dancing and singing, waving their heads, throwing their hands up. At the height of this I had been more aware of movement and mass, particular parts as opposed to whole human beings, but now I was more here, aware in a more conventional way. It was communal and perfect, and I was now also more aware of tripping itself.

I had a feeling that I was presiding over all this. For an instant, I thought I might go out and preach, as I have seen a few mentally ill homeless people do, from the gospel of kindness I had glowing inside me. *Look at the bricks*, I would say, *and the colors, and know, children, that God is here with us.*

The sun and clocks were telling different stories, and this—how can I explain it?—began to bring on the first pangs of a spiritual dread. I tried to hide, but I wasn't sure from what. Then I got stuck in the bathroom.

You can imagine how a bathroom would look at a Lollapalooza. There were people getting high, vomit and watery feces and urine on the floor and walls. But none of this bothered me. What did bother me—the urine feeling electric coming out of me, like long, solid, charged strings being yanked from me by an unseen force—what got me stuck, was all the cigarette butts. Then I started thinking about the person who had to clean up. In my mind, it wasn't a squadron of cleaning people; it was just one little woman who walked around with a bucket—a bucket of sorrow, a bucket of shame. I began to weep. I did.

Standing in front of the urinal, I became obsessed with this woman, this imaginary, symbolic, oppressed woman, whose job it was to clean all this mess up, and how she probably wasn't capable of handling a job this big. Where were the pamphlets, the mass mailings, and the booths for this woman, I wanted to know. Who would start the custodial revolution? Who would speak for the single anguished soul?

With tears abseiling down my cheeks, I looked over at the guy next to me and said: Hey, someone has to clean this up so try to be careful with your spray and pubic hairs.

I felt that pubic hairs, in particular, were cruel things to subject this lone woman to, a woman who now, in my mind, had just left an abusive husband and had five, no, six hungry children to feed, all somehow under the age of three.

He stared at me for a few seconds and then nodded. I was red and sweaty, and I hadn't showered in days. He might have slugged me had I not been crying, looking like a serial killer.

The day changed. The light changed. The tone changed. It was still good, still beautiful in a whole new way, with everything opened up to me for what it really was—or so I was convinced—but I was coming down.

Night was falling. The sky couldn't totally darken because of all the stadium lights. Jane's Addiction came onstage. I went up to the top, where the steep grassy hill met the concrete, to watch.

I didn't know where any of the people I came with were. Perry Farrell brought out two women dressed in S-and-M outfits, and they were rubbing on him in a choreographed way, and the music was getting faster and faster, and he was shouting about Ted Bundy and fucking and the lies and exploitation of the media, and I was sweating still and feeling a little faint, a hunger moving through me.

Suddenly there was a guy with long hair and a T-shirt with a pithy beer/sex double entendre. He asked if I was all right and I replied that I was—why wouldn't I be?—not realizing for the moment that he had pulled me up off the ground where I had been lying passed out.

When it was all over I was completely and utterly lost. I started getting a little worried about my friends then, thinking that they might have left me, that they might have seen me lapping the stadium with my giant eyes and my foul stench and become scared of me. I walked down the hill toward the gate and the parking lot, the muscles in my back and legs beginning to hurt from the earlier flipping.

As I said, before the trip I had been thinking about all the ruin around me, family problems, all the kids I knew who were getting busted, wrecking cars, becoming different, desperate people all of a sudden (that was a big part of why I went driving, rather aimlessly, around the country). Now these thoughts resurfaced, stronger than ever. And when I looked around after the show, my head roaring from the long day of loud music—the intensity of feeling from the height of the trip still lingering—I started noticing people, kids, lying in their own puke, or a big guy getting all over a sixteen-year-old girl on a towel who was just seconds from passing out, or two guys pushing each other, their faces close together, their mouths open, barking like feral dogs.

There was no epiphany, no bright holy light, no real moment of wonder. Just the feeling that I was in need of an ending. I wiped my eyes and tried to remember where we had parked.

gray
world

*L*isten: locked away, he began his education. He had time now to learn, after years of avoiding it. It was written in the letters I never answered. He was full of knowledge.

He learned math in a classroom the color of slate, chalk squeaking out numbers and signs on a blackboard. An old man, an inmate, a man who did something illegal to his own children long ago, sweated and talked about theorems, formulas. Numbers, in the abstract, he found difficult. The old man, he wrote, was smart but a bad teacher, full of water and ideas and terrible secrets, unable to fully share even mathematics for fear of revealing a dark part of himself. He worked hard, though—to learn, to understand all the basic things he'd ignored throughout his life, to prove some-thing. At lunch he counted men the way children count apples or spotted cartoon dogs. He learned that two men were most likely able to overpower one, that three men could always overpower one, no matter what you might hear, and that it was better to be one of the three than the only one.

In wood shop he made a clock, a battery-run, working clock he was proud of, that someone smashed when he wasn't looking. Then he made a shiv out of a thin piece of PVC pipe and electrical tape for when he found out who smashed his clock, which, I believe, had come to symbolize, in some vague way to him, his progress as a human being, his ability to do things people on the outside might consider productive. He needed to kill the fucker who crushed his human progress. He stabbed some-one he didn't like, hoping that he was the crusher of human progress. But it was the wrong man. Inside, these things happen. All is flux. The right man and the wrong man are the same man; it's all about in-tention and revenge, the means not the end. Some-one deserves it; someone gets it; if they're not the same someone, who really gives a fuck? For this he slept in a dark room for forty-five days, until his eyes were glued shut and his lips were cracked and his skin was the color of the squeaking chalk the old man used for the theorems. He counted the days in cold, soupy meals.

In the letters he misspelled the crucial words. He spelled "niggers" with one *g* and "spicks" with an *x*. I found myself fixing some of his letters before putting them away—an old habit. P.S., he wrote, please write me back. Please. Loneliness is the worst disease, because it is survivable. He used the word "please" like a weapon. I hated him the way you can only hate someone you love.

He learned quickly that blacks hated whites and whites hated blacks. A fact, like natural law. There was no compromise. A compromise would get the white compromiser killed by the rest of the whites. The same was true for the blacks. Hispanics, however, were different; depending on their skin tone they could go, occasionally, either way, if they knew the right people, although mostly they stuck together, too. It was different in the West, he had heard, where there were more Hispanics. But in Virginia, he wrote, the spix are few and can go either way. Many didn't even speak English. Inside, he wrote, it would not be bad to be light brown. It would not be bad to not know the language, which was a language of senselessness and violence and ruin. He longed, I imagine, to be unidentified, lost, invisible.

He also learned, slowly, to read and write. Just a few years ago. In his thirties. Then came the letters, in a killing flood. He wrote all the time, to me, an old girlfriend, his mother, filling up our desk drawers, boxes. He wrote and wrote and wrote, manic with the power of language, roaming back and forth through his whole life, remembering, inventing, reinventing, shaping, trying to articulate, looking . . . He read the Bible. It was the only book they'd give him; it was the only title he could remember. It took him a long time to read it, but he found it both cryptic and intoxicating. So he read it again—and again and again . . . Later, he felt God in his fingertips and was sorry for so many things that he could not stop crying. He lived in a sorrow you can only find in a dark place without freedom, a place where time meant everything and nothing and space was a myth passed around for comfort.

He learned that Jesus Christ was crucified for our sins and that on the third day he rose from the dead. He liked that, rising from the dead. He liked the idea of Heaven, he wrote me, of just dropping your body and moving on. He liked that the end of the Bible became dark and cautionary—a bad dream, a bad trip—warning of a preordained end to us all. He said he liked St. John as much as Jesus, maybe more. He said he knew Judas, and Paul, and that

Job, an ex–auto mechanic, constantly paced around, beating on his bars. The Bible made him feel small. It was so big, so beyond him. He professed his love for God, which helped, but only some. He had been an empty vessel up to now, he wrote, misspelling the words, and now he was ashamed.

As a Christian, after learning about the death of the body, of all bodies, he did not so much mind the things he did. He had learned early on that it was best to choose—as much as one was able to choose—a group of men that you did not mind having sex with. This way, he learned, sex was paid for by protection from others that might want to have sex with you. He learned to give himself to a few to be saved from the many—he thought of this in instinctive mathematical terms. He learned that he was probably not a homosexual but was capable, in certain circumstances, of acting convincingly as one. He learned one day that being raped was a terrible, violent, humiliating thing but that fighting it often made it worse; fighting it made it all violence and no sex; pretending was the way to go; pretending was self-preservation.

He prayed every night. His asshole bled. He never got an erection again, never, he wrote, even when he fantasized about women, the ones that seemed almost fake, the ones from magazines with giant breasts and white-blonde hair, those plastic female Americans that went about making themselves for the sole purpose of fucking, the ones that used to work for him every time, the ones that now turned into smiling men right there in the middle of his head. He had become, he wrote, a woman, a whore. I am becoming plastic.

He cursed God and then apologized. He bit his lip, tasted blood, thought, *I am still real. I am still here.* It wasn't him they wanted to destroy, he reasoned, staring at a ceiling that was the same cold color as everything else; it was his body, and the body, he had learned from Jesus Christ Himself, was temporary.

He learned, then, to cooperate, sacrifice.

He learned from a priest, the same man who taught him to read, that having killed another human being (pointlessly and intentionally) considerably lessened his chances of being saved. It doesn't just happen, the priest told him, you have to work. His last letters are about the difficulty of being saved.

He needed to work harder than he could.

His body was so tired.

He learned, when he was exhausted, that drinking cleaning fluid was not good enough, that they could pump your stomach, bring everything up in a blue stream. He learned that it was hard to leave your body in here if they didn't want you to.

You did not own your body in prison.

Nothing belonged to you.

Nothing had worth.

You were plastic and you could be melted down for materials.

Please, he wrote me, please write back.

I own boxes full of pleading. I own a man's heart in pencil marks.

He learned that a belt, even if you could get one, was not the best thing; buckles are made of different pieces, and different pieces, as a rule, eventually come apart.

The last thing he learned, after so much trying: the soul is light, infinite, and always glowing; the body, this life, a burden.

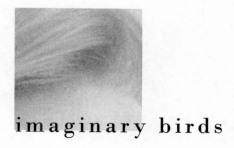

imaginary birds

O nce upon a time, an old woman lived two doors down from a young writer, in a place where violence, of one degree or another, happened every day, a place where the young writer himself had been mugged for six dollars, where the leather-clad homosexual living above him had been beaten so badly that he had to be fed through a tube in his nose for a week, a place, in fact, where the old woman's son, the writer learned one day, had been murdered for no discernible reason while jogging in a park (he didn't have six dollars or his wallet with him, wasn't even wearing a leather biker hat or chaps)—and all this woman did now, as far as the writer could tell, was stand on her stoop, two doors down, which was

Greg Bottoms

in a line of stoops all basically identical save for the
colors they were painted—stoops that dated back
to Civil War reconstruction—and smile a crooked,
left-veering smile because of age or perhaps a certain minor palsy that had wrenched her face
slightly to the right and frozen it there, forcing her
smile to kind of head left, just like that, charmingly
crooked, so when she spoke to people walking
by—anyone would do—she was always smiling
with a beautifully deformed face when she said,
*Hey you, there, young man, do you hear that, do you
hear those beautiful birds singing their song,* and the
young man, of course, who in this particular instance was the writer and who, perhaps because of
a certain unwillingness to let himself go completely
insane just yet, didn't hear any birds—or it could
have been because of the very simple fact that there
were no birds anywhere near there, not real ones
anyway, not even a pigeon, a filthy pigeon trailing
a line of gray-speckled shit across the statues of
dead people whose names had all been forgotten—
but this young man, the writer, stopped anyway
and looked at the woman and the woman looked
at him, smiling, and he smiled back and listened
even harder but still all he heard was traffic and a
little wind and a distant car alarm screaming at itself
like someone in a locked ward, yet as he stared at
her—her bent, old, broken body, her hands like

gnarled roots, her long, white hair curled up on her head like, he actually thought this, a small cat—he decided to play along because he wasn't in any hurry, being unemployed and just getting over a mild but still serious little problem with his mind, so he said that he did hear them and he thought maybe they were mockingbirds, and she said, *No no no*, they weren't mockingbirds—*mockingbirds?* she said—but rather songbirds that sang so beautifully that there wasn't even a name for them yet, so there was no way to talk about them at all, you just had to sit on the old stoop and smile and listen closely and be very still and open yourself up to the song, and so the young writer—still staring with his mouth open—and the smiling old woman, who happened to be crying now, leaned close together on a street where it was not really safe, particularly after dark, which was on its way (falling, right now, down the face of dirty brick buildings), listening to a song by birds that were so beautiful that they didn't exist or have a name, and it was then, right then, at dusk, with the light a strange blue-purple, that the writer saw, in the back of the old woman's eyes, the tiny black reflections of birds wheeling about in the sky.

intersections

Urban renewal is ripping the cracked and withered face off of downtown. Jackhammers and big orange signs. Dump trucks and workers loitering in intersections. Someone was elected (the bus driver looking through his vertical, convex window at the rutted street below can't remember who) on the promise of a new face, a makeover for this sagging section of city. Right, thinks the driver. Just picture it: spit shined and sparkling. Pinch and tuck and tighten. Put up new signs, cut taxes, offer some kind of small-business loan to anyone daring to open a shop. Make the cops move downtown and have cook-outs with the crackheads. He's a bus driver, drives these streets every day, knows this town from the inside, this bus like a blood cell cruising the pocked, asphalt veins; he knows. Knows better, is what. You can do what you want—legislate, promise, procrastinate, lie. Probably doesn't much matter. But damn, how about fixing the potholes?

The bus driver (African American, 46, 6'1", 227 pounds and on a diet because of prodding from his wife, stomach rumbling *at this very moment* and nothing in his lunch box but carrots and rice cakes) has driven this road, crossed and recrossed this grid of city blocks—not far from where he grew up— four times a day, five days a week, for fifteen years. Not a bad job, driving. All right, maybe it's a good job—benefits, decent salary, retirement plan, the whole bit. Of course he'd quit if he could, sure. It's a job, not a career. Got to feed the family, got to make the bucks, but that's not what fills your heart, man. No, not exactly for the soul, this job, but not bad for the soul either, that's not what he means, just, you know, *soulless*, he thinks, coming to the seventh stop along his morning route, air brakes doing that *squeak whoosh squeak ssss* he knows so well, hears sometimes in his dreams. Singing. That's what he'd like to do—have someone pay him to belt out a tune that would turn you into a puddle of tears. Now church choir fills the heart, is good for the soul; watching his son play baseball, how he can knock that ball into space; and his daughter, too, bringing home straight-A report cards—that's the stuff, family— his wife's liquid eyes, her silky hair, the curve of her sweet-smelling neck where he likes to softly place his lips, so softly. He likes going home at the end of the day and not thinking about a big machine: engine going like a sick cow, gears popping, stony faces floating in his mirror. And the hemorrhoids—don't even get him started on the hemorrhoids! Let's say he won the lottery—*if I won the lottery*—won maybe a modest ten million, which works out to be about five hundred grand a year. First thing he'd do, after vomiting on his shiny standard-issue black shoes, would be to quit. Not even pick up his last check. Say to the boss, *Keep it, buy yourself something nice.* Then he'd get his family, light of his life, three human beings he loves so much that sometimes just thinking about them brings tears to his eyes, everything they wanted. New car, new baseball equipment, new teachers, new schools (his daughter makes straight A's in a school with metal detectors and a couple of murders a year, so many assaults that the school board had to get tougher on how they defined "assault"). And at his seventh stop (a stop he has made approximately 15,000 times in the last fifteen years), as the door accordions open with a mechanical sigh, as he lets on the street preacher who smells of rancid meat and urine, smells of rummaged-through restaurant Dumpsters and puddles of pickled wino piss, he knows that, with that cool ten mil, he'd move as far from this place as possible.

The preacher (an emaciated guy with a matted red beard and long hair the color of soot) steps left right left up the bus stairs, knowing that right left right will hurl the universe spinning toward a disaster. (Every day he gets on at the bus driver's seventh stop and rides six blocks, gets off then to walk six blocks, then rides a final six blocks to a place where he stands and attempts, loudly, to untangle the infinitely intricate puzzle of the last days on Earth: These Days. He repeats this pattern at the end of the day exactly backward, always taking the steps left right left to keep the universe from spinning toward a premature disaster; he's got enough to think about without that on his head.) Preacher likes the bus. Comfortable. Gives him time to read, think, make notes in the margins of his Bible on top of layers of other notes. (He's been thinking about good and evil for more years even than the black bus driver, whose name he does not know, has been driving this bus. He graduated from a prestigious Southern university twenty-five years ago. And then, certain moderately concerned people said, he just lost it. He doesn't remember those people—friends, lovers, teammates, roommates, colleagues—the people who said things like *just lost it*, although occasionally one will show up, make a brief cameo in a dream. They often have fangs and spit like exotic poisonous snakes.) He's devised some theories. Considers, now, a couple of Psalms—singsongy, poetic, they burn his fingers when he touches the words. Good and evil exist together in the world, in each of us, mixed, or, no, that's not what he means, not mixed, but on top of one another, yeah, oil and water, in the same murky puddle, the puddle being us. It's the comfortable same, the bus (there is divine peace in routine; protective angels live in the familiar movement, the practiced gesture): same time, same faces, same route and scenery, same flesh and metal smells, same drone and squeak of engine and seat, same soft sibilant sounds of quiet talk: whisper whisper whisper whisper, keep it all to yourself, put a lid on it, shake it up, motherfuckers, whores, cunts. He knows what they're saying, God knows what they're saying, and not saying, those little secrets like rotting teeth in their mouths, what they take to bed with them and wouldn't breathe out, wouldn't let foul the air, even in the dark. Same everything. Same every day. A leaning hotel, a beautiful woman, a shiny car, a packed diner with glass skin. A store, a group of boys (baggy pants, expensive shoes, cigarettes), bicycles. Streetlights, a corner, an alley, an empty lot where weeds strive from the cracks in the concrete. Good and evil, love and hate, weeds and concrete, the same murky puddle—us. (Notes on top of notes.) Empty lot gets him thinking (gets him scrawling like a polygraph—lie lie lie!), feeling the crackle and pulse up his spine. A bum was found there, a guy he sort of knew, bound in electrical tape and beaten deader than dead, dirt and trash and cigarette butts stuffed into his mouth, tiny red burns covering his face and neck and scalp and hands. Covering his hands like stigmata. People heard things, television said, but people always hear things. Lambs. A stop. Man gets on. Woman gets on. Child gets on, a girl. Seat beside the preacher's empty. They know who he is. He's got their number. He reads their dreams like delicate scrolls. Good and evil, oil and water, same murky puddle, us, weeds and concrete, dirt in his mouth, tiny red wounds. Driver looks at him, big black guy with the glare in his eye who thinks he knows God because he hangs a cross from the mirror, because he bows his head and gets herded into church Sundays like an idiot beast for slaughter. Black guy looks at him in the mirror, looks, cheap cross swinging like a dog dick. *Religion is pounds of flesh and bottles of blood, brother,* he wants to shout. *If I were as weak a Christian as you, I'd divorce myself from life* (he read that somewhere). Doesn't speak, though; chews his fingernails instead. Six stops later, gets up, takes his bag and Bible. People turn, look, know who he is, know he can save them or destroy them with the tiniest beat of his heart. *I forgive you*, he says to the driver (as he does every day). *Thanks*, says the driver (as he does every day at the thirteenth stop). Door sighs its tired sigh. Preacher gets off, left right left (to walk the six blocks). Day unreels. Skyline blurs. Lamps hang their heads. Good and evil, oil and water, the same murky puddle.

Girl catches an elbow in the biceps. Big mouthful of that stench before she can speak, like a dead animal, that smell, fresh and dead, entrails still on the road, or like that guy in the VA hospital where she volunteered when she was a teenager, the fat one with like fungus or mold growing under the folds of his breasts, maggots in there before he was even dead, like that, something dead or dying. *I'm sorry, Miss, forgive me*, says the old guy. (The preacher spends sleepless days and nights at a time pondering religious notions of forgiveness.) Backing away, feeling the pinch and pucker of her face, muscles cinching up in the stink, and taking a long, deep whiff anyway. *I forgive you*, she says, walking on, stepping away, breathing in deep the air away from him, the clear, perfect air, rubbing her shoulder where she knows a bruise will form (she bruises easily). I forgive you, she thinks, what a weird thing to say, even to a rotting homeless guy. Ought to say that to her mom. Yeah. Walks on, heading for the store. To get Velveeta cheese and pasta shells; two bucks and you have lunch and plenty left for dinner; or maybe just soup and a loaf of bread, the good wheat kind with the chunky little grains in the crust, probably not even real grains, sawdust or something, just decoration, but still, good stuff, good decorative stuff. Guy almost broke her arm, that's for sure. She needs a sling or something, an ice pack. *I forgive you.* What would Mom say to that? I forgive you for not understanding graduate school, for not even being interested in painting, for making her talk about things that don't interest her so they can still do the mother-daughter chat. She loves her mom, even if she drones on about her father working all the time, and playing golf on the weekends, and never being interested in sex, or at least rarely. Always wants to lay some heavy stuff on her about sex and an older woman's needs, all tinged with that New Age stuff she reads. Mom says that most women find cunnilingus an arousing form of foreplay and a way to become functionally more lubricated, *especially* as you get older. Her father used to be into that sort of thing, used to be a real muff-diver. He

never went down on her anymore. Always, at
some point, Mom makes it around to her leaving
this part of the city. Every time. From uncomfortable sex talk with the woman who breast-fed
her, changed her diapers, put her hair in pigtails,
told her how pretty she was after she got dumped,
to what a bad idea it is to live in the city and go
to that school, and how there is bad energy in the
economically challenged parts of cities. Wishes she
could explain, in one coherent breath, explain how
it's important to her to understand deep aesthetic
theories of painting and art, and to know the history and progression and movements of art, understand that art is, as she once read somewhere, a
finite sphere and how the artist, the serious artist,
must know, in her own particular way, that sphere
and then hope and work and sweat to create something that can survive on the outer edge of that
sphere and, hopefully, make that sphere grow as it
must. Art. Spheres. That's what she's thinking
about at this very moment as she walks. Spheres.
Making a living is sort of beside the point. It's
teleologically bohemian rather than professional.
Can't say something that stupid and pretentious to
her mother, after trudging through the whole cunnilingus spiel. Damn frustrating: She's sensitive to
the desperate condition we humans find ourselves
in. Wants to be an artist more than anything.

Doesn't want to *sound* like she wants to be one.
Wants to sound like she just naturally is one. Very
cool. Very understated. The kind of artist people
are always going on and on about but also the kind
that never, ever, never wants to talk about her own
work, its complexity, its depth. Aloof. Mysterious.
Yeah. She gets trapped in this circular stuff, trapped
thinking in grand arching metaphors and trying to
get her mind around big thoughts. Or maybe
they're really really small thoughts. She doesn't
know. But she's not leaving. That's for sure. (Later,
if she becomes that artist she hopes to become, she
may attempt to dispense with the intellectual pre-
tensions and find an honest, earnest, centered place
from which to work and incorporate into her art
everything she has ever known and felt, a much
harder task, which may drive her to feelings of
failure and futility, to stiff drink and thoughts of
suicide.) Her work has improved in the city. She
sees it in the brushstroke, the poetry of one motion
leading to the next, feels it in her formal control.
Her vision, whatever that means, has broadened
and deepened. She knows this. Sure, she's become
more aloof and meditative, like her mom says, like
her friends say, more brooding and temperamen-
tal—all those clichés are true. And she reads too
much, looks at paintings too much. But she's doing
her best work. Like her new painting, *The Rape*,

in which a girl walks to a corner store, like she is doing now, as two men, decently dressed, nonchalant, whisper behind her back. Best thing she's ever done. A year ago, *The Rape* would have been more overt, less evocative and subtle and dangerous (here is her nascent art vocabulary), without angry brushstrokes suggesting menace in the calmness of the scene. No, in that big house outside of D.C., she would have shown the rape explicitly, blood and gore and ripped clothing, or with painfully bald metaphor—the men would have dicks for noses and chubby little dick fingers holding thin, burning dick cigarettes—she would have lost everything, bored herself. Violence, orgasmic, finalized violence, has become passé. Not life. Life is scary. But she doesn't want to be clumsy, or obvious, isn't even interested in being accessible or commercially viable. She wants, instead, to be deep, to be subtle, like Woolf and James and Rhys and Joyce—like that, art like a perfect little dream, all interior, all suggestion, all implicit. She walks; she strides. Her painting, in a certain way—in its intention, at least—is probably better than Caravaggio's painting of the same name, which focuses on a perpetrator, evokes empathy for all those driven to steal another's soul while desecrating the body (she read that somewhere). Her painting evokes sympathy for all involved, for the tragedy of living in a world full of fear, for perpetrators and victims, for the forces that make people either one or the other. All these men around here, dirty, lost men looking her over. She gets the creeps, paces around her apartment at night, rechecks the window locks, the dead bolt on the door, keeps a couple of lights on all the time, a phone by the bed. *The Rape* is a painting in which she faces her fear, tries it on like a comfortable pair of jeans, a painting in which every brushstroke contains a terrible sadness and beauty, a painting full of the sounds of distant gunshots and sirens and drunks and careless, broken people chattering in her skull. A painting as calm and dangerous as downtown at sunrise or dusk. Walking into the store, smiling at the clerk, she is thinking these things, how being here and watching people and the feeling of danger and low-wattage rage that lives in the concrete and steel and mortar and blank faces has given her something she didn't have before. *I'm scared to death, Mom,* she will say, *I'm so alive here that every scene, every tableau, every defeated glance, reminds me of death.* And I've never been worse. And I've never been better. And I forgive you for things you've never thought about.

She gets some food, just a can of soup. Lost her appetite on the way. (This happens when she really gets to thinking.) Pulls a wadded-up five from her jeans. Hands it to the clerk. He unfolds it and, holding it in both hands, rubs it back and forth along the edge of the counter to straighten it before giving the girl her change. Attractive girl. He's seen her a few times. Probably stuck up, like the rest of them. The clerk doesn't, as a rule, talk to the grad students around here, with their little beatnik glasses and requests for overpriced wines, with their big talk and expensive clothes made to look worn-out. Closes the cash register (smiling, falsely, at the young artist he doesn't know is an artist). Construction is killing him. That's the thing, or one of the things (one of the things that makes him the cruel, sad person he is). No one can even get down here, unless they come from the east. The people with the money come from the west. Two dollars and twenty-nine cents in three hours. His whole life has been a constant worry over money (he often says these exact words to his wife), over crumpled fives and inventory and big chain groceries just blocks away that can afford to buy and sell everything and especially the kids from this neighborhood who come in here and steal him blind. The money he makes from the old guys, he tells his wife (the yellow-eyed men buying Thunderbird and Mad Dog 20/20 and quarts of malt liquor and lottery tickets), he loses to the little thieves. These kids, these little fatherless, twentysiblinged kids. Little thieves, bred to take and take. Welfare turns women into Chia Moms—just add water, or better yet wine, and they drop a litter, swear to God. These kids. Kids everywhere. Like the one he notices as the smiling grad student leaves (thinking those grand depressing elliptical thoughts about art and life that he will never talk to her about). Like that kid, the black one with braids or locks or whatever the hell these people call this hairstyle. Walking around like he owns the place, picking things up, putting them down, labels facing backward, upside down, he doesn't care. None of them do. Watches the kid, maybe, what, fifteen, sixteen, ought to be in school in the middle of the day, as he picks up and puts down, opens coolers, wasting expensive cold air. Strutting, browsing, probably doesn't even have any money. You going to buy something or not, he says loudly.

Kid looks at him. Me, kid thinks. Walked in here a minute ago, maybe two. Been wondering about the white girl, the one that walks around talking to herself like she doesn't know it's dangerous around here, walks around at night. Walked in here with half a mind to tell her she needs to be more careful. Knows, though, that a black kid walking up to a white girl, a student, saying how she ought to stay in at night, be careful, wouldn't look right, might spook her more than it helps. (And now he's looking at the clerk framed there behind the counter by two video monitors, one for outside, one for inside.) TVs behind the clerk like a pair of eyes. Sees himself, a black wavering line in the middle of the left eye; sees himself seeing himself (a pre–convicted criminal living on tape). *Yeah, I'm going to buy something. Is there a time limit for black people?* Fuck this old guy, looking at him like a thief, watching the nigger like a hawk because all niggers steal, fuck him (he, the kid, has stolen, in his entire lifetime, a Schwinn bicycle on a dare, several of his sisters bras to play a joke on a friend, and numerous candy bars). Ought to steal something. Old motherfucker. Ought to round up all his brothers, a whole mess of scary black folk to hurl fried chicken and watermelon and curl activator and crack vials at your window, racist motherfucker. *Sign says no loitering,* says the old clerk. *Buy something or leave.* Says it real slow, like for a stupid person. Kid can't believe it, gets treated like a criminal in his own neighborhood because he doesn't have his hands in the air and his pockets turned inside out. He wouldn't give this man a penny, wouldn't piss on him if he were on fire. Cool, composed, kid says he doesn't see anything he wants, puts his hands up. (And it is only as he walks out, as he puts his hand on the thick glass of the door, leaving five perfect fingerprints, and the man says something under his breath, that the anger, those hard little bubbles of hate in his throat and in the pit of his stomach, take over.) Puts his hand on the unsteady magazine rack by the door, yanks it (one small act of aggression and release, almost thoughtless, the slightest twitch of the arm; and *right now*, elsewhere in the city, other acts of aggression, both small and large, misdemeanors and felonies, just and unjust, random and premeditated, are also happening). Spills the metal and the magazines along the floor, glossy covers sliding over the greasy white tiles behind him. *Club*, *Hustler*, *Penthouse*, *Vibe*, *Ebony*. Kid wants to slap the old man in the face like some whiny, spoiled child. But he is in a flat-footed sprint down the block already. Knows better than not to run, knows he needs to get down one of these alleys and out on another street because a nigger running around this neighborhood will be picked up sure as shit. Turns the corner onto Main (having no idea that it is the next leg of the bus driver's route), legs pumping, and hits the big fat white woman like he's hitting a brick wall. Puts her large and hard on her ass. Watches her bounce.

Woman feels a small rock embedded in her right butt cheek. No pain yet, just numbness, shock. Kid says sorry, kid says sorry oh my god let me help you up, kid says, you okay, you all right, and is gone, sprinting, bobbing and weaving along the crowded sidewalk, shouting as he goes, *Really sorry!* This has been her day. (If this were six months later and she was taking that night class at the university in an effort to become a matriculated student at the age of thirty-four, she would say that this incident was a physical manifestation/representation of the crappiness of her first day in the city. She does not, however, think or say this now.) Standing up, she counts to ten as people step around her. I'm fine, she thinks, looking up, thanks everyone for not stepping on my face. She counts. Counting calms her down, an effortless sort of meditation (it's how she keeps from hitting her daughter sometimes, counting). Keeps her from yelling what's what at that goddamn black kid. (She moved in with her sister last night, into a loft just a few blocks away, so she could find a job here, because she lost her job of six years at home and figured the city was the best place to come to find a good job. So far she's filled out five applications, two for waitress positions, and been flat turned away at three other places—and then she gets knocked down walking to the bus stop.) Eight . . . nine . . . ten. This has been her day. Remembers her two-year-old daughter throwing food all over her sister's kitchen this morning. Almost threw it back; she wanted, she ached, to dump the whole mushy meal over her daughter's head (she can't believe how hard it is to be a mother). She would have done it maybe if her sister weren't there. Walked off, though, counting. Looked in the bathroom mirror. Thought how she wouldn't hire herself because she just wasn't pretty enough, and so fat. Fat fat fat. Then she thought of her daughter. Then she thought of wanting to dump food on her, how cathartic that would be. How evil that is. How beautiful her daughter is, just a baby. How she doesn't know better. Remembers, now, how she sat on her sister's toilet with her insides just a churning mess because she was nervous about the job stuff, bawling like a child as her daughter sat in the other room rubbing food all over her face, cooing that puzzled, beautiful little coo. This has been her day. Guy a block over, preaching and screaming into the crowd, some kind of Bible in his hand with writing all over it, looked right into her eyes while he was talking about sodomy and "vitriolic dykes." Big-boned, okay, but not gay. Walking, sidestepping people on the sidewalks, she takes in the city, looks at it, breathes it, tastes it, how different it is from home, the hilly Virginia countryside. Everyone here has a blank face. (Her anger wanes, as if disappearing into the noise and odd-smelling air—hot asphalt on a southern breeze—and it is replaced by a funk, a deep, bone-chilling funk that anyone, if they were looking, could see take shape on her plump face.) She stands at the bus stop, afraid of sitting. Rock feels like it's still stuck in her skin. People are staring at her, staring at her back, seeing how huge she is, or whispering about her, the fat lady, the fat dyke who abuses her child, who doesn't love her beautiful child. Everyone, every face, is a chiseled stone, their expressions so rigid, the cold eyes afraid of betraying what's beneath, which could be anything: a killer, an angel, a fool, or just the shell of a human, like the husks of cicadas stuck to trees back home. (And her own face is like this as she looks, catches eyes, looks away, though she doesn't think about it.) Bus stops. *Squeak whoosh squeak ssss.* Bus driver swings open the door (he's still calculating his lottery winnings after taxes and setting up his extended family: his mother in a rest home, his brother in Georgia, his favorite uncle Donald and so on). He stares right into her eyes and smiles and says, in a musical baritone, *Heeellloooo.* She smiles—*my bus driver sounds like Barry White*—wants to thank him, wants to tell him how he really saved her, how a hello at the right time is like water in the desert, which would be stupid and melodramatic, she realizes, especially here. (He is smiling because next stop he gets to

take his lunch break and he's thinking about getting rid of the carrots and rice cakes and getting
something of substance, but she doesn't know this,
and takes it, the smiling, personally.) She sits in
the seat nearest him, her eyes meeting his in the
mirror.

levi's tongue

*F*amily records—culled from hearsay and gossip, shaped by myriad imaginings, a hundred-plus voices easy, each adding and deleting, shaping and reshaping, veering the narrative this way and that—lead me to believe that this story takes place on the last Sunday in June 1902, sixty-eight years and five months before I am born. Already there are questions of veracity. Even before the beginning. But I will go with that, the hearsay, the speculation, the family record: a final Sunday, June 1902.

The weather has just broken after a week of heavy, black-bellied storms. Two hurricanes—

Agnes and Bertha—have recently brushed the North Carolina coast, washing fishing trawlers and crab pots and cracked, orange buoys and pieces of stranger's front porches and dead livestock and family pets forty miles up the Chowan River.

The river is bruised and swollen. The sun flickers through the treetops, as if unsure of its power, a white hole poked in the sky. Birds perch in the willow and roughed-up pine trees, squawking about their vanished nests, looking down at the flotsam and dead things speeding along on a backward-moving current, on a river running from the sea.

My great-grandfather, Levi, is three years old today. Levi will grow up to be a popular Methodist minister in Chapel Hill, North Carolina, and the husband to four wives over the final thirty years of his life before he dies of colon cancer, before his insides sour and rot and his body caves in around them.

Right now, however, he is healthy, running, infantile, beaming blond and top-heavy like an apple on short stilts, keeling forward toward the water, along the shallow, sandy slant of the river's bank.

He is laughing and laughing because life, for now, is only this: this running, this laughing, this happiness. Life is cool water and a big sky; life is the meaning of a word you can't remember, the smell of people in a bed, a soft touch. Other things, too—a blur of life behind him—but these things foremost: a sound, a scent, the brush of skin against skin.

He is plump and speechless and naked. His penis, which some will later say led his life more so than God Almighty, is the size and, because of an oddly out-of-season brisk north wind, hue of a smallish unripe grape.

He is the boy at the center of the world, the reason the sun shines and the sky is blue and dogs scratch themselves with their backs bowed and ears cocked and birds build nests of twigs and feed-bag scraps and catfish flop onto docks bubbling with black muddy moss and you taste pennies with the top of your mouth and his belly button sticks out instead of in and his poo is sometimes hard and sometimes soft and smells of molasses and mother's milk; and he is the reason that other people, all these people around today, even bother to exist, to breathe this humid air.

He is running past all of my variously aged and shaped family members in turn-of-the-century eastern North Carolina. They are not ghosts yet, or daguerreotype images, or blurred memories in need of a narrative; they are gathered near the splintered wood picnic tables sagging under the weight of food: fried chicken, greens with lard and ham, bean salads, corn salads, fried soft-shell crabs, cakes and pies.

There is laughter among the women near the tables as they repeat the gossip of their churches, exaggerated tales of the promiscuous and the virginal.

The men are more somber, serious, gathered under the shade tree near Levi's father's summer cottage (torn down in the 1960s and replaced with the cottage still sturdily standing, the one I visit every year, the one that houses the family records—kept in a large box in the attic—that are the basis of this story). The fishermen from the Outer Banks and the Currituck Sound complain about the weather, about lost bait pots and boat repairs and the labors of barnacle scraping; the farmers of the eastern plains complain of flooded crops and tobacco prices and their "lazy niggers"; the clergy—of which there are at least five of various Protestant denominations at this time—complain of souls straying from the glorious, mysterious wishes of God.

Cousin Jeb, a twenty-something-year-old seminary student and son of a noted Scottish Anabaptist evangelist, is telling a group that the "scientist" Darwin and the "Yankee intellectual" Emerson were indeed emissaries of Satan, complicating the truth,

confusing the Word. The fishermen and farmers of
my family, having no idea whom he is talking
about, and frankly not caring, heartily agree, shaking their heads while sipping moonshine-spiked
lemonade.

Today is the second baptism of Levi.

Through the picnic, toward the river's edge, a
commotion: Levi's father, the Reverend Harold, is
chasing Levi, angry, impatient, no time for this.
But Levi doesn't understand his father's anger—
this is only another game—his rages and dark
moods, his supplication and genuflection in the
morning before dawn and his curses at his wife at
night.

Later, decades later, Levi will write in his un-
published memoirs: *My father was two people; we are
all at least two people.* He does not have the capacity
or sadness to think this now, however.

Caught up suddenly in the giant hands of his
father—this is how he will remember it, how he
will tell it—Levi floats, weightless, through the air,
down the coarse, sandy shore. He is giggling. It is
a game of chase and he has lost. His father's face
is red and silly. His father's face is a stupid, silly
county-fair balloon.

Harold calls everyone to the river, calls for
"brothers and sisters in worship." It is time. De-

spite the trees bowing in the wind, despite the angry river—in the near distance, you can just make out the bloated carcass of a cow—it is time.

He turns Levi over, carrying him like a package. His shiny black Sunday shoes blur beneath Levi, making a faint squeaking sound in the fine sand. Levi hears the wind and the crickets and the steady hiss of the river; he hears the talk stop around the picnic tables as the family—fifty, sixty people— head down to line up along the Chowan's reedy shore for the ceremony.

The men and women gather along the bank— women to the left of Levi and his father, their husbands and sons to the right, as if arranged in imaginary church pews—leaning on the willow trees bent over the wide river like things about to drink. Up higher on the bank, some little girls and Nanny Newby and Great-Granny sit in the green, stiff grass, under the woods' canopy, swatting bugs; a few of the girls lean toward each other, head touching head, and pretend to pray while playing a secret game called "guess my thoughts" that Great-Granny taught them for when they were bored and had to be quiet.

A lone tenor voice rises. Everyone begins singing, singing hymns, and for a second, Levi thinks, the hymns are the wind and wind is made of church hymns.

Levi's eyes are filled with the colors of the family. Everyone is dressed in their finest suits, the men in small white hats with colored bands—blue, red, black—the women with bigger hats, all of them white, their faces shaded, eyeless in shadow, their mouths open and singing. There are bright dresses and white shirts, white gloves and fans waving and suspenders and the shine of the river blinking on polished shoes.

He is still smiling, though no longer laughing. He puts out his arms when he sees Great-Granny, but she looks down at her hard black shoes and kills something on the back of her neck with a fast open hand.

Levi is above the water now, wobbling a bit in his father's hands, as if trying to catch his balance, and he feels the water's stormy coldness, the different air above it. Bits of wood debris race by. Great-Granny not looking at him frightens him. The girls having their heads together frightens him.

His smile bends into a frown and he starts crying. He shits and the mess slides warm and liquid over his small buttocks, down his legs, over his father's hands, into the steady-moving water.

Reverend Harold, exasperated once more by the child, passes him to Uncle Reedy, who is also waist-deep in the water.

Reedy, a fisherman, holds him in his cracked,

callused hands, saying, *Ah nah, ah nah, Levi, don't you go an mess yusef.* Reedy has hands even bigger than Harold's, rock-hard and pitiless, and Levi cannot move.

A few amens from the shore.

Harold stands in front of Reedy and the crying Levi, an open Bible in his hand. The sleeves are rolled up on his white shirt; his black suspenders and a black tie, loose at the throat, are splashed with water droplets; his torso cants left, or north, because his feet are braced on the loose river bottom. Around the Bible, his hands are cracked and wet and almost purple from the cold water.

Harold begins shouting, not looking at the words, just shouting. *Out demons, out sickness! I come bearing witness, to bear witness to the light, that all men through me might believe!*

They are here, for a second baptism of Levi two and a half years after his first, because Levi hasn't spoken a word in his three years, has barely made a noise beyond crying. He doesn't mumble or coo, but rather runs and walks and pauses and stares. The blank staring—at roots, at bugs, at boats, at the sky—has become a worry to his father. His mother, my great-great-grandmother Olivia, worries, prays, talks to him, and reads the Bible to him through most evenings as he stares blankly up into her face, watching her mouth move, the curve of her nose, her crinkled eyes. They know he isn't deaf because he looks when you call his name. He is afflicted by the spirit of silence, and they must ask God to cleanse him and cure him of this.

Levi's brothers—Harold, Jr., who will die in the war from a bullet through his brain while cleaning the mud from his rifle in a French trench, and Barnaby, who will drown next summer in an odd fishing accident involving moonshine and a fish-net—leave him sitting on the porch for hours, go off to the penny store or fishing, knowing Levi won't cry, won't scream, will just sit in the yard with red ants crawling in his dirty diaper, sweat bees and wasps buzzing by his ears and then back up into the drooping willow trees. He'll sit staring out at the daylight as a water moccasin esses its way under the outhouse. He'll watch donkey-drawn work carts throw up road-dust clouds. He'll watch field mice scurry under the porch, a stray dog lick-ing himself out in the dirt road, going to sleep, almost whining, in the relentless summer sun. His sister, Emma, who will die of the flu during the epidemic of 1918, dresses him up like a cornstalk doll because he can't tell and he doesn't seem to mind, corn silk drooping over his ears as he smiles and shakes his head, a pretty little girl.

But his father, the respected reverend of the First Baptist Church of Little Washington, the singer,

the evangelist, has seen the signs, the signs of Satan
in his young son, the signs of endless speechless-
ness, of secret thoughts, of sin, which will, he
knows, grow and fester as he ages. This isn't just
a baptism today in the river, this isn't just Harold
shouting on a Sunday afternoon again about the
glories of God Almighty, the accepting of Jesus
Christ our savior into the fragile human heart; it is
balm for Levi's spirit, an offering to the Lord, and
a request to save the boy.

And the lord, Harold is saying, *will claim you for
his own. Will show you the light and the way!*

The family along the banks—from toddlers to
the elderly, all of them now long dead—give an
amen, and some of the men and boys in their suits
walk down into the water now, and Levi, above
them all in Uncle Reedy's hard hands, watches the
reflections of their upside-down faces smeared over
the fast current. Sunlight falls through the leaves of
the bank's trees like water through a colander,
making flickering points of light on the river's surface.

Harold finishes his sermon and prayer. He and
Reedy nod at each other and trade—the Bible for
the boy.

Harold takes a tight grip on the back of Levi's
small neck and around both feet, keeping him
faceup so he can dunk him backward. The women

along the bank are all standing, swaying their arms above their heads.

When Levi goes under for the first time, everything vanishes, the song of the people and the wind and the crickets and the birds and even the sound of the river. (When he is *in* the river, the river seems to vanish.) He hears only the echo and gurgle of a strange void, an emptiness. The sun is a blue jellyfish above the massive rippling shadow of his father.

He slams through the surface and into the air, gasping and screaming. His father holds him high above the river, at the end of his outstretched arms, up into the sky, pleading before God to save the boy, please save the boy.

Singing and clapping from the shore. Amens. Levi sees Great-Granny, who died later that year in her sleep, with her arms raised and her eyes closed and the toes of her shoes in the water. Reedy is reading slowly, full of effort and mispronounced words, from the Gospel of John: Let not . . . your heart . . . be troubled . . .

When Levi goes down the second time, he hears only his own heart sputtering, echoing off the river-bottom rocks, from where he sees the minnows flee. He passes into a different place, it seems, a quieter place like sleep but not sleep. He is down a long time, maybe a minute, but he doesn't struggle in his father's big hands. Even at three, only half-conscious of the world, he trusts his father completely, and if his father sees fit to kill him here and now in the cold Chowan, then he will die. He opens his mouth.

He breaks the surface and flies high into the air at the end of his father's reach and his chin scrapes up against the clouds and he feels the too-close heat of the sun on his skin. He takes in a breath and he feels as if his chest has split. He can't make out his father's or Reedy's voices anymore. Every voice is one voice and a part of the swaying of the trees and the hiss of the river. Blue spots hover before his eyes. He tastes some new sickness and feels his body emptying of everything.

When he goes under the third time, his body turns limp in his father's hands—this curious boy, this walking and wandering child with bright blue eyes, eyes, my grandfather once told me on this very beach along this very river, exactly like mine—his arms moving downstream with the motion of the water.

From high above the trees Levi watches himself come loose from his father's grip, his father trying to reach out for him and missing, wading fast through the water, missing, swimming with the current, throwing out his hands, missing. He sees himself—a small, white object—speeding on the current.

While he is above the world, watching himself, he dreams he can hear the voice of Reedy reading from the Gospel of John, the voice of Great-Granny praying in her head. He dreams he can hear the thoughts of the whole family along the bank and the men diving into the current. He dreams he can hear the thoughts of his swimming father, feel his fear: *No no no.* He can hear the trees and the rocks burning in the sun and the grass sizzling in the wind and thunder from the storm two states away that will hit tomorrow night. He can hear the world's heartbeat like a snare drum, and it is deafening. He dreams he can breathe under water, so he does.

Then everything is silent. All his dreams turn to black, and his small body turns blue, and he gets tangled in the branches of a storm-downed tree.

Levi's father and Reedy and his mother and Great-Granny are standing in the cottage (not far, I imagine, from the very spot where I am standing, where cobwebs hang in the corners), on what seems the worst day of their lives, the day of Levi's death.

Levi is lying on his father's bed, under a blanket, his face covered up to the bridge of his nose. Harold is wondering if it is more painful to hang or to drown. Olivia is rubbing her child's chest through the material, tears sliding down her face. She is repeating the word "no," though Harold has already told her to shut up once so he can better concentrate on how to kill himself.

Uncle Ed (Edmund, not Edward), an alcoholic veterinarian who will kill himself in 1911 with the ether he uses to put horses under, pronounced Levi dead about half an hour ago. Levi's body was the color of an old bruise. He wasn't breathing and had no pulse when some of the men pulled him from the water, bleeding from the minor abrasions and punctures in his flesh.

When Levi begins to cry and cough, everyone jumps back. Uncle Reedy runs out into the front yard screaming. Great-Granny soils her best Sunday drawers before fainting. Harold drops to his knees and thanks God, pulling Olivia to her knees on his way down. They kiss the ground. They kiss each other. They kiss the suddenly warm feet and hands of their child.

Levi stares quietly at the ceiling, still tasting the brackish water. This, his eyes opening into a new life, will be the opening scene of his memoirs, as well as the beginning of his most famous sermon, which he will repeat thousands of times in many different churches throughout North Carolina. Some versions of this story have it—and I am inclined to believe these versions—that he used this, his "resurrection story," to seduce women. Without this story, it could be argued, my grandfather may never have been conceived, and thus my father, and thus myself, and thus this story—at least this particular version of it.

The famous family reunion of 1902 winds down later that cool summer evening, while stars turn on like a million electric bulbs and the full moon finds its place just above the trees of the river's other shore, with song and praise. Levi stands on a tree stump, in his best Sunday suit, eating Aunt Edna's famous lemon cake and smiling as the whole family stares at him in wonder and a little bit of fear. Levi rose from the dead and they all witnessed it. No one is sure what this means, what this makes young Levi, and they are unaware, of course, of what a lying, hypocritical, womanizing preacher he will become, how he will use his knowledge of the Bible to advance his own life at the expense of others, how he will leave three women and eleven children and fool even himself into thinking he is a good Christian.

But they are superstitious, my family (even I am superstitious, I'm afraid). For all they know, at that moment, he's the Second Coming of Christ. And Levi, during several mildly psychotic episodes during his life, particularly toward its sickly, palsy-stricken end, will believe this himself. In a Raleigh nursing-home bed, in late 1968, with crusty sleep in his eyes barely holding back his tears, and slobber on his chin, and tubes in his nose, and skin like tracing paper, Levi will often repeat the phrase: "I am a man of God. I am a good man."

This evening in 1902 ends, as every family reunion before or since, with the whole family joining hands in a circle and bowing their heads in prayer. Harold begins by thanking the Lord for his family and for giving him his youngest son back today. He asks for mercy for his carelessness in the water. He pauses, begins to weep.

Levi, without warning, without even a clearing of his small throat, splits the dark silence by uttering his first two syllables: *A-men.*

The family, my family, all long gone now, just memories and ghosts in the corners of this cottage, take off sprinting into the darkness, and each one of them—all of these people running through the brambles and brush, screaming for their Lord, *please, Lord, save me*—will remember this day in a slightly different way, and tell their version of it to their children, who will tell their children, and so on, until, after so much repetition, this story will transform, like a fable in our religion, from a questionable anecdote to good gossip to compelling myth to the irrefutable truth housed in a musty attic.

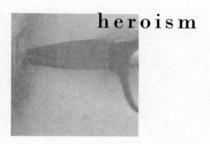

heroism

I was parked in a vacant city lot, sleeping in a company truck, when the fat homeless man stuck his head in my window.

I worked as a legal courier, generally messing up the preferred whereabouts of vital contracts and documents. I'd smile at secretaries in important-looking offices—the kind with regal portraits on the walls and real hardwood floors and paneling and soft classical music piped in from hidden speakers—right before they said things like, *Oh, this isn't us, honey, this is the other firm, the one across town.* I was always floating around, thinking about some masterpiece I was going to write, my mind worked over by the ten-hour days and the driving

and the thick diesel fumes and the unblinking sunlight. My incompetence startled even me.

—Hey, said the man, his face eclipsing the sun.

I sat up, open-eyed, let out a little scream that
had been crouching in my throat for weeks.

—I went to high school over there, he said,
pointing out at the city. He said this with the soft,
raspy intonation someone more mentally stable
might use to say, *I am in love.*

—Oh, I said, calmer, thinking now that he
would simply ask me for change. —That's interesting.

Several of his teeth were gone. Shatters of blood
vessels spread across his meaty nose. One eye was
half shut. There was either dirt or a big grayish
birthmark on one cheek.

He had been a star athlete in high school, the
one out there in the ether that he kept pointing
to. That seemed to be the gist of what he was
saying.

Eventually, he asked me for a ride. The radio,
the one they used to chastise me for botching de-
liveries or taking too long, wasn't barking any
commands. I said, —Sure, get in.

He smelled, frankly, like he'd soiled his pants a
week or so ago and hadn't bothered himself about
it. His belly nearly hit the dash. I think the spot
on his face was a birthmark. Or cancer.

—Where do you live? I asked.

—Down there, he pointed.

I followed the direction of his finger. —Where?

—Down there, he pointed again.

He was pointing to an alley entrance strewn with garbage cans on the other side of the vacant lot. It was about fifty feet away.

—That's where you live?

—Yeah. For now. I'm looking around, though.

—You want me to give you a ride over there?

—Please. You'd be saving my life, man. I can't walk across the lot with the sun like this, and all those weeds, man, growing up through the cracks. I'm stranded.

—You're *stranded*?

—Isn't that obvious? Look around you, man. I mean, just take a look! Christ!

His face quivered like water. He seemed like he might cry. I couldn't take that, him crying in my truck. I felt a little quivery myself. I rolled over to the other side of the lot, near the alley, at about five miles per hour. He tensed up, cringing, as we rolled over the sunniest part of the asphalt.

He got out. He thanked me over and over, as if I'd given him one of my organs, or five pints of blood. I rolled back over to the other side of the lot and tried to nap again until the next call, which could be an hour or more around lunchtime. I sat up to look a few times to find him standing there in the shade, mumbling to himself.

Over the next six months, until I was getting ready to go to graduate school, every time the man saw me pull into the lot to nap with my radio hissing pickups and drop-offs, he would waddle out of his alley, just to the edge where building shadow met sunlight, and fling up his hands in victory signs, as if I were some great hero returning home, as if I'd actually saved his life by giving him a ride across fifty feet of hot asphalt.

I was having a hard time back then. I'd lost a lot lately. My loneliness resided in the dead middle of me, like starvation. I'd drive miles out of my way to see that fat homeless man; to fall asleep, on the clock, a hero.